A HORROR NOVEL

J.A. KONRATH
TALON KONRATH

GRANDMA?

January 2017

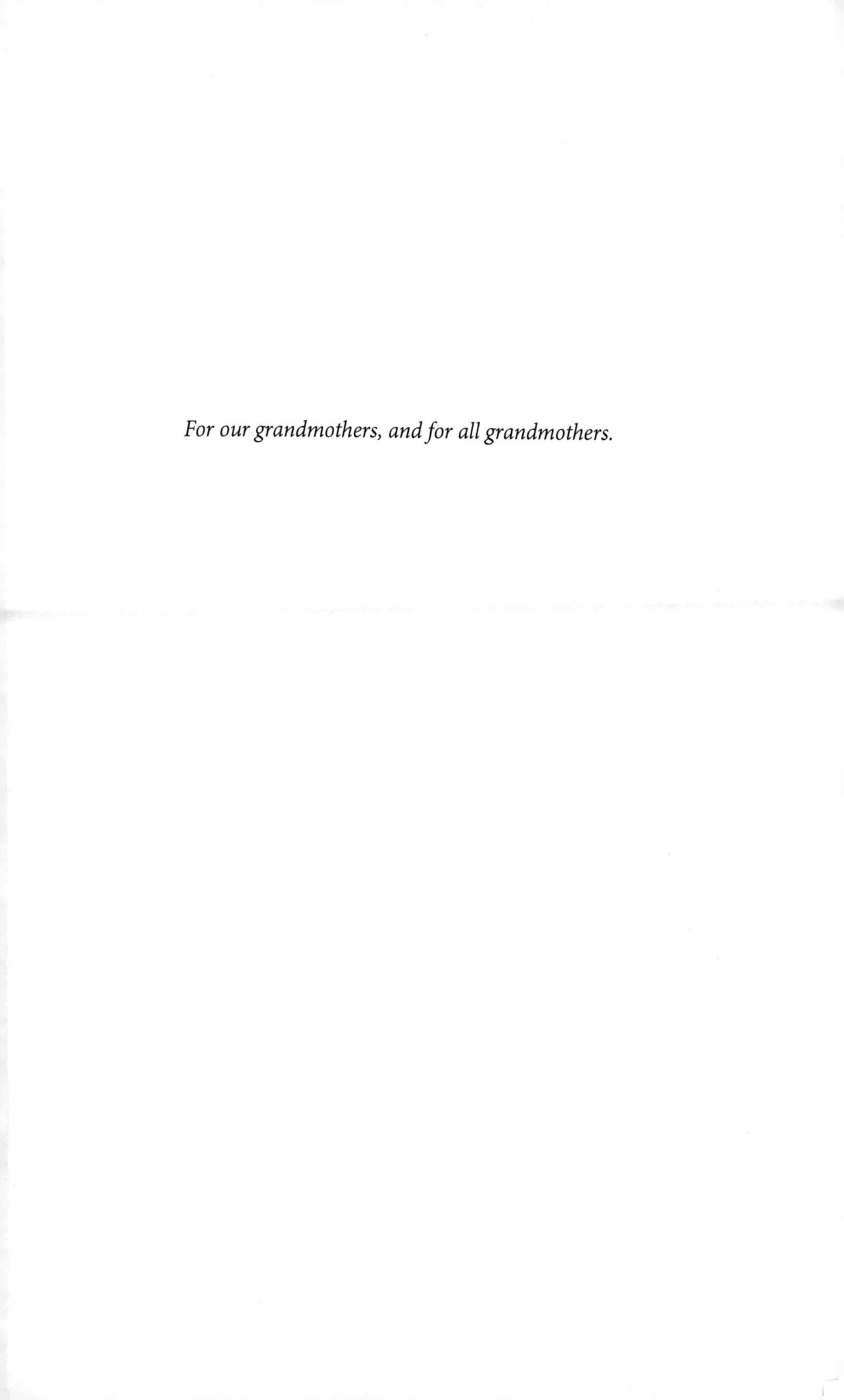

For our grandmothers, and for all grandmothers.

A Cabin in Northern Wisconsin…

“Is Grandma gonna be okay, Randall?”

My brother’s brown eyes were wide with worry.

Grandma’s brown eyes were fixed on the ceiling, her hand pressing a towel against her bleeding throat. She wore a dark blue housedress with a yellow flower pattern, the upper half soaked through with red. Blood also matted her hair.

So much blood.

I stared at Josh—seven years younger than me and about to start third grade. He was sitting on the floor next to Grandma, cradling her free hand in his. A minute ago he’d taken a throw pillow from the sofa and put it under her head. There was a streak of crimson across the kitchen’s hardwood floor from when we’d dragged her into the house.

“I don’t know, Josh.”

We continued to watch her breathe.

Inhale.

Exhale.

Inhale.

Exhale…

Her chest stopped moving. Josh squeezed her hand, his knuckles turning white. I felt my heart count the seconds.

Grandma's eyes stared off into nothing.

"Grandma?" Josh brought her hand close to his face.

I knew CPR; I took a class at the YMCA while Josh futilely attempted swimming lessons. But Grandma had a hole in her neck. If I blew into her mouth, wouldn't the air just come out of the hole? And if I pressed on her ribcage, wouldn't that just cause more of her blood to come out the wound?

Inhale.

It was a small, wheezy gasp, but it proved she was still alive, and it was enough to stop Josh from squeezing her hand to death.

"Randall? What happened to her?" Josh's wide eyes had become wet and glossy.

I didn't know what to say. I couldn't tell him what I saw happen while she was gardening. I still didn't believe it myself.

"She, uh… she fell on her shovel. You know how old she is."

I turned away, unable to look at him while lying. Instead I picked up Grandma's cordless phone on the floor next to us and heard the recording.

"All circuits are currently busy, please stay on the line…"

I pressed the button to hang up and tried 9-1-1 again.

Same thing. What the hell was wrong with emergency services in Northern Wisconsin?

"Are they answering?" Josh asked.

"They put me on hold."

"Did you dial wrong?"

"It's 9-1-1, Josh. That's pretty tough to screw-up."

"Let me try."

I handed him the phone. He dialed and listened.

"What the hell is wrong with emergency services in Wisconsin?" he asked.

I nodded. "I know, right?"

In all fairness, there had been a big forest fire in the area a few days ago, which affected parts of Lake Niboowin. Maybe emergency services were still dealing with that.

But there was no excuse at all for the hold music.

"Ugh," Josh said, holding the phone away from his ear. "Smooth jazz."

I nodded again. My brother and I didn't agree on a lot, but we *were* related, and sometimes it felt like we could read each other's minds.

"Smooth jazz sucks," I said, grateful to talk about something other than the tragedy that was unfolding before us. "It's like a bunch of musicians forget what song they were playing, so they just keep playing scales."

Josh set the phone down, sucky smooth jazz playing faintly in the background as we stared at Grandma and wondered what we were supposed to do.

"When are Mom and Dad coming back?" Josh asked.

"Soon."

Another lie. I had no idea when they'd be back. When they went hiking, they were sometimes gone all day. Sunset was still hours away, and there was very little cellphone reception at the cabin. Mom had taken her purse, which had the car keys in it, and Grandma's car was in the shop.

When my parents got back, we could get Grandma to a hospital.

Josh stood up. "I can go to the neighbor, ask for help."

"No!" I thought about the garden. What I saw.

It wasn't safe to go outside.

"We need to get help, Randall."

"You just want to get away from the smooth jazz."

"I know you're trying to use humor as a tension breaker, but if we don't do something soon..." His voice trailed off.

"I can find help."

"We should go together."

"You need to stay here. Keep pressure on the towel."

His eyes widened. "Don't leave me."

"I'm not leaving." I touched Josh's shoulder. "I'll be right back."

"Pinky swear."

"Pinky swear."

We locked our little fingers and shook. Then I stood up.

I didn't want to go, but I had to.

I didn't want what happened to Grandma to happen to me and Josh.

So I left the kitchen. But before I tried to find a neighbor I began to check every door in the cabin. The backyard. The patio. The front door. The garage.

All locked.

Then I checked the windows.

Upstairs bedrooms…

Locked.

Bathroom…

Locked.

Kitchen…

Locked.

Living room…

The brown curtains fluttered from the cool, lake wind.

The window was open. Open wide enough for a man to fit through.

I stared for a moment, my mind exploding with possibilities.

Could *he* have gotten in the house?

Fear shocked me into motion, and I ran to the window, shut it hard, clicking the locks in place. Then I hurried back to the living room.

"Okay, Josh, I'm going to—"

Grandma and Josh were gone.

My heart went into overdrive. The towel was on the floor, blood staining the wood where she'd been laying. But there were no more streaks. Grandma hadn't been dragged away.

Grandma must have gotten up.

The phone was also back on the cradle. Maybe we were wrong, and Grandma's injury wasn't that serious. Maybe she was actually okay.

"Josh!"

No response.

Where the hell were they?

I raced back upstairs.

"Josh?" My voice not as loud as before.

The silence allowed me to hear my heart pounding in my ears. I waited for noise, for any movement.

Then the floor creaked. It came from the bedroom Josh and I shared.

Someone was in there.

"Josh?" My voice shrank to a whisper.

I walked down the hall, trying to be as quiet as possible, and placed a sweaty hand on the doorknob.

Another creak.

Was it Josh and Grandma?

Or was it something else?

The thing I was afraid of?

Chill out, Randall. Just open the door. You can do this.

I pressed on the door, opening it an inch—

—and heard something squeak.

It wasn't the wooden floor. This was something different. Almost like a bird chirping.

Be Nike. Just do it.

I tugged the door open, raising up a fist in case I needed to punch, revealing…

An empty bedroom.

"Josh! Where are you?"

The silence mocked me.

Squeak.

My ears told me it was coming from inside the room, but nobody was there.

Squeak.

It was a familiar sound. And close. But I couldn't place it.

"Grandma?" I whispered.

I waited for the squeak to come again. As I did, my eyes scanned the room. No windows were open, so it couldn't be the wind. Maybe it was just a chipmunk or…

Squeak.

The closet.

The door was closed, and the squeaking sound was coming from inside.

I'd always been afraid of the closet, even though I'd never admit it to Josh. One time, when I was his age, Mom and Dad took us to visit Grandma. I kept all my fishing gear in that closet. I'll never forget going inside to get a pole, walking right into a giant spider web—one swarming with hundreds of little baby spiders that had just hatched. They crawled all over my face, into my hair and ears; me screaming and slapping and smearing spider guts all over my head.

From then on I kept my fishing stuff next to the bed.

I stared at the closet door, my hands at my sides, not wanting to open it.

Squeak.

The sound was definitely coming from inside.

"Josh? That you?"

But why would Grandma, or Josh, be in there?

Squeak-squeak.

I wanted to run. I wanted Mom and Dad. I wanted this to be a bad dream so I could wake up. I wanted to be older than fifteen, so I would know what I had to do.

But the truth was, I *did* know what I had to do.

I had to check the closet.

I patted my hip, feeling for the Swiss Army knife I always carried. Except I wasn't carrying it. Josh and I were wearing swimsuits, and my knife was still in my jeans.

Do I get the knife, or open the—

Squeak-squeak.

Maybe it was Josh in there. Maybe he was hurt.

Hurt by the man that hurt Grandma.

My hand reached out for the closet knob, moving in slow motion. A cold drip of sweat ran down my forehead, stinging my eye. I took a huge breath and exhaled nice and slow.

It was probably nothing. I needed to stop being such a wimp.

Then I threw open the closet door—

—and saw the crazy old man who bit Grandma's neck standing there, Josh's bathtub rubber duck in his mouth.

He chewed on the toy, the yellow plastic mottled with Grandma's blood.

Squeak-squeak.

His eyes were milky white, crinkled at the edges in apparent glee. He slowly reached out his arms for me, and I saw his neck also had a large bite on it, so deep I could see the black, squiggly veins. His sweatshirt was splattered with blood, some of it dry, some still wet, obscuring something—a name tag—hanging around his neck.

I stood there for a moment, feeling like I had to pee, and then terror made my muscles move and I slammed the closet door shut.

The man—or whatever it was—began to squeak the duck again.

I stepped back, unable to breathe. Unable to run.

Squeak-squeak.

I needed to get away. But my body wasn't listening to my brain.

Squeak-squeak.

Squeak-squeak.

Squeak…

Then the closet doorknob began to turn.

My muscles were all locked up, and my feet felt like they'd grown roots. I watched, lungs petrified, unable to scream, as the closet door creaked open.

The duck fell from his mouth, and his jaw opened impossibly wide.

He was going to bite me. Like he bit Grandma. And I was just standing there, like a deer in the road, staring at the approaching headlights, too shocked to move.

"Randall!"

It was Josh. He sounded far away, but hearing him snapped me out of my frozen fear. I gasped in a breath, and my legs began to move by themselves, racing me out of the bedroom and into the hall, toward the sound of my brother's voice.

"Josh! Where are you?"

"Randall!"

I sprinted downstairs, back to the living room.

"JOSH!" I screamed.

C'mon Josh, where the hell are you?

My eyes scanned the room. No Josh. I flew into the kitchen.

"Randall!"

Basement. It sounded like he was in the basement.

I tore down the hall and flung open the basement door. It was about twenty concrete steps down, into a pit of darkness. I hit the light switch on the wall, but it didn't work. I was supposed to have changed the light bulb earlier. Dad told me to, three times. But I was fishing off the pier and had forgotten.

"Josh?"

"Grandma's okay! She can walk and everything, Randall!" Josh's shrill voice rose through the black. "She can bake us her chocolate chip cookies like she always does, the ones with the Hershey's Kiss in the middle! She can work in the garden again, just in time to harvest her cherry tomatoes! Grandma's okay!"

Josh was creeping me out. He sounded hysterical.

"Josh? You all right?"

"Come down here, Randall!"

I took a step down, squinting, seeing nothing.

"Grandma?" I called.

"She's standing next to me!" Josh said. "Come down!"

I should have been rushing down there. Rushing down to Grandma and Josh, and then getting them out of there before the man in the closet got us. But it was really dark, and I was freaked out.

"Grandma?" I called.

Grandma didn't answer.

Flashlight. I needed a flashlight.

"Josh, I'll be right there."

I went back to the living room.

Where the hell did I put the light? I had it yesterday when Josh and I were collecting pine cones for a pine cone fight. Did I leave it on the couch?

I pushed the cushions aside, checking the inside of the sofa. There was a Cheeto—God knows how old—a quarter, that missing red checker we'd been looking for, some crumbs. Then I went to the kitchen and began opening all the cabinets and drawers. I heard something and paused. My ears sharpened to—

Is someone giggling?

My search quickened, shoving aside glasses and plates. Hands shaking, I found a box of light bulbs.

Screw the damn flashlight.

I hurried back to the basement door, clutching the light bulb box. The darkness giggled at me. I couldn't tell if it was Grandma or Josh or…

Or that zombie from the closet.

I wasn't stupid. Zombies weren't real. They were make-believe, like vampires, and honest politicians. If I had to take a guess, it was a serial killer in the closet, wearing zombie make-up to scare people. Or some lunatic who actually thought he was one of the walking dead.

But he couldn't be a real zombie.

And he couldn't have gotten down in the basement so fast.

Right?

I squinted into the darkness.

"Josh?"

My brother didn't answer.

I took a step down, and the giggling stopped. I stopped, too. I pulled my cell phone out of my bathing suit pocket, using the blue screen to see ahead of me, a foot at a time.

I took another step.

One more.

My arm waved above my head to feel the ceiling for the dead light bulb.

There!

I quickly unscrewed the dead bulb, but I went too fast and it fell out of my hand.

Oh no…

The light bulb bounced on a step, then shattered on the basement floor with a telltale tinkling sound.

I winced. I wasn't wearing shoes. My flip-flops were out on the pier, and my gym shoes were in the bedroom.

It'll be ok. Just be careful.

I pinched the new light bulb from the two-pack cardboard case and carefully screwed it in. Then I felt along the wall for the light switch and flipped it on, anticipating the nice glow of a white light.

But it didn't turn on.

I flipped the switch multiple times.

No light.

I reached up, making sure the bulb was in all the way. Bad bulb? Problem with the socket or switch?

I should have looked for the flashlight instead.

"Randall?"

It was a whisper, so soft I couldn't tell if it was Josh. Or Grandma.

Or someone else.

I'd heard the term 'made my skin crawl' but didn't know what it meant until that moment. It meant you felt like you were covered with bugs because you were so afraid. The hairs on my legs, arms, and neck all stood up and wiggled. If the closet zombie was downstairs, I'd wet my pants.

But it could have been Josh or Grandma, needing my help.

This was, officially, the worst summer vacation ever.

I shook off my nerves and forced myself to act.

Ready or not, here I come…

I used my phone to light my descent, testing the stairs with my toes. I did NOT want glass in my bare foot. I remember when Dad got a large piece in his heel after breaking a picture frame, and he had to go to the ER where they used a scalpel to dig out a whole chunk of his foot.

The stairway light didn't work, but there was another switch at the bottom. One that flooded the whole basement with nice, bright fluorescent light. All I had to do was make it down five or six steps.

I kept my hand on the left side of the wall as I went down.

One step…

Two…

Three…

"Randall?" It sounded like Josh.

I blew out a breath. "Yeah, it's me. Turn on the lights."

He didn't respond.

"Josh?"

"I… I can't."

"What? Why?"

He didn't answer.

"Josh, turn on the frickin' lights."

"Grandma said if I do, she'll kill me."

I paused for a second, replaying the words in my head.

"She said what?"

No answer.

"Grandma?" I said, louder.

I heard some whispering, but neither one replied. I took the next step and—

CRUUUNCHH.

Glass shattered under my right heel. But I was careful enough to not step on it hard, so it didn't penetrate the callus.

I took another step and I felt the texture under my feet change from wood to cold cement. I used my phone light on the left wall and found the switch. I flicked it on.

A flash of white light blinded me for a moment. I squinted until my eyes refocused.

Then I saw Grandma and Josh, standing in the corner of the basement. Josh was holding Grandma's hand. Grandma was as blue as her dress, her face looking like death. Her neck wasn't bleeding anymore, and her eyes were milky white. She didn't speak. She just stood there, swaying back and forth.

My mouth went dry, and my bladder felt full to bursting.

"Gra… Grandma?" I whispered.

She stopped swaying, and tilted her head. Her neck cracked several times, like a bag of potato chips when you squeeze it. She squinted her cloudy eyes at me.

Then she let go of Josh's hand and screeched.

It didn't sound like Grandma.

It didn't sound human.

I couldn't process it mentally, but deep in my gut I knew the truth; Grandma wasn't Grandma anymore. She was something else. Something that wasn't going to give me a big hug and a plate of cookies.

Something that looked at me like *I* was a cookie.

She charged at me, much faster than an elderly woman should have been able to run.

Even though I couldn't believe this was happening, I backpedaled so fast I landed butt-first on the stairs. Scrambling to turn around, I forgot about the broken glass and stepped on a chunk of jagged bulb, the pain screaming up the arch of my foot as I charged upward.

Grandma screeched again, louder than before. I snuck a quick look behind me and saw she was doing a bear crawl up the stairs, just a few feet away. I freaked out so badly that I tripped on the steps, falling onto my chest. I turned quickly around, the stairs poking my back, and Grandma climbed on top of me, smelling of blood and Elizabeth Taylor White Diamonds perfume. I arched, trying to shove her off, but she was impossibly strong, her bony hands pinning down my arms.

Her red mouth stretched open—

—and clamped down on my neck.

I cried out, crazy with fear and disgust, getting a hand free, shoving her away.

Her false teeth slurped out from between her flappy, pale lips, and plopped onto my belly.

I pushed against her shoulders, keeping her away from me, while her cold hands patted down my body.

She found her teeth, and shoved them back in. Then she smiled.

"How's about a kiss for Grandma?" she said, in a voice straight out of Dante's Inferno.

Then she went for my throat again. I put my hands around her neck.

"Grandma! It's me, Randall! Stop!"

Grandma didn't stop. Her mouth opened wider and a long rope of pink drool came out, landing on my cheek. I managed to bring my knee up, and I kicked her in the stomach, knocking her down a couple of stairs. Then I crab-walked up the last few steps and shut the door. There was no lock, so I pressed my back against the old wood, wondering what to do next.

Squeak-squeak.

Oh no...

I looked up. The zombie from the closet—I was pretty convinced by now that both he and Grandma were real honest-to-god zombies—was standing in the hallway, staring at me. He'd put Josh's rubber ducky back into his mouth and was gnawing on it. But now he also had something in his hands.

Grandma's BBQ fork. The long, sharp one she used for grilling hot dogs.

This can't be happening.

The door creaked behind me, Grandma trying to get out.

The old man began to shuffle toward me, fork raised.

I had zero desire to be the next item on the lunch menu, so I ran into the living room, looking for a hiding place, spotting the linen closet. I squeezed inside, shelves pressing against my back, and pulled the door shut just as I heard the basement door fling open.

"Raaaan—dall," Grandma called in a deep, sing-song voice.

As my eyes adjusted to the darkness, I noticed a tiny crack in the door jamb. I peeked through it as Grandma lurched into the living room.

"Would you like some hard candy, Randall?" She reached a claw into the pocket on her house dress, what Josh called her *candy pocket* because it was always filled with peppermints or butterscotch drops. "Come give Grandma a kiss, and you can have a piece."

She dug out a handful of candy, the wrappers stuck together with blood. I held my breath and my bladder as she walked up to the closet.

"It's naughty to hide from Grandma," she said, saliva slick on her wrinkly chin. "You don't want to make Grandma angry."

Then she paused, staring at the floor.

"Naughty boy, Randall. You messed up Grandma's clean floor with your blood."

She dropped onto all fours like a cat, and a liver-colored tongue snaked out of her mouth and lapped it up.

I quietly felt around on the shelves behind me, my fingers curling around a familiar spray can of room deodorizer. I gripped it tight, my finger on the trigger, as Grandma followed my bloody footsteps, one by one, toward the closet door, licking as she crawled.

"Tastes like snips and snails and puppy dog tails," she said, reciting an old nursery rhyme she used to sing me to sleep with. "And it left a nice trail right........... to........... you!"

She yanked open the door, squealing with delight.

I sprayed her in the face with McGlade Brand Air Freshener.

"Nooo!" Grandma cried, her arms flailing. "That's six dollars a can!"

I let her pry it from my hand, and quickly stepped around her, heading for the sofa. The cushions were wrapped in clear plastic to protect the fabric, which I always hated because they would stick to my bare thighs. But as I picked up the middle cushion I was grateful for the extra support, holding it out like a shield between Grandma and me.

"Put that down, Randall," Grandma ordered, waggling a finger. "No rough-housing on the furniture."

She sounded almost like her old self, and something inside me broke. My eyes became glassy.

"Stop it, Grandma. Please. Just stop it."

"I can't stop it, Randall. I've changed. You have to accept it. Change is inevitable. Look how much you've changed. You were once a sweet little baby, so tiny I could hold you with just one arm. But you're not that little baby anymore. You're different. So am I. I'd like you to accept that. Now put the cushion back on the couch like a good boy and LET ME EAT YOU!!!"

Grandma lunged, and I braced myself, forcing her away with the cushion, and then ran for the patio door to find a neighbor and call the police.

"Randall!"

My brother's voice made me stop before running outside. Josh was still in the basement, and he sounded hysterical. I couldn't leave him.

"There's a man down here!" he screamed.

I looked for the zombie from the closet, and he was gone. I'd been so focused on Grandma I hadn't seen him go down the stairs.

"Josh! I'm coming, buddy!"

"You're not going anywhere," Grandma said, spreading out her arms like a football cornerback. "Except in Grandma's tummy."

Then she charged at me. I charged, too, running full speed into her. We connected and the impact knocked her over the kitchen counter, her slippers flying off, her false teeth coming out again, skittering onto the plastic rug runner, stopping next to a cabinet where she kept the bird feed. Grandma cupped her mouth, then scurried after the dentures, and I ran to the basement stairs, descending them two at a time—

—my bad foot landing on the broken bulb again, making the pain double.

Biting back a scream, I hobbled into the basement and searched for my little brother.

"Josh! Where are you?!"

The basement wasn't that big, but I didn't see him. I didn't see the old guy, either.

Where could they have—?

The laundry room!

"Josh!"

I limped across the concrete floor, and opened the door to the laundry room. The old man was poking at the dryer with his fork.

"Hey!" I yelled.

He looked up at me, the duck in his mouth squeaking. I thought fast.

"Walmart called," I said. "You got the greeting job. It starts today."

He spit out the rubber duck and made a face. "I fought in 'Nam, sonny. Private Gustav Johnstone won't take no pitiful minimum wage."

"Thank you for serving our country, Sir. But you shouldn't be trying to eat me."

"You smell like tater tots, boy. And tater tots are meant for eatin'."

Then he thrust his fork at me. I dodged to the right and the points scratched my cheek. Then I used his momentum to push him out of the room, slamming the door behind him, propping the ironing board under the knob.

Josh was where I guessed he was; inside the dryer. He was sobbing. I put my hand on his shoulder, and he shrieked.

"It's okay, buddy. It's me. We're safe in here."

But as zombie Gustav began to bang on the door, I lost faith in my own words. Both the door, and the ironing board, were old. They wouldn't hold up to too much pounding.

I helped Josh out of the dryer and hugged him tight. His whines grew louder with each pound on the door.

BOOM!

I could feel it in my teeth.

BOOM!

The door's hinges strained, two screws popping out.

BOOM!

The ironing board began to buckle.

BOOM! BOOM!

Two booms. Grandma had joined the zombie party.

"Randall! Josh! It's bedtime, put on your jammies!" she crowed. "Grandma will tuck you in and read you a story!"

"*Wuthering Heights*!" Josh said, trying to stand up. "No, *Jane Eyre*!"

"Shh," I told my brother, holding him back. "That's not Grandma, Josh."

"Then who is it?"

"It's…"

What was I supposed to say? That our Grandma had joined the ranks of the living dead and wanted to feast on our flesh?

"Has Grandma become a zombie?" Josh asked.

"I…"

"She wants to feast on our flesh, doesn't she?"

I didn't answer. But sometimes I felt like that kid could read my mind.

"I thought zombies weren't real," he said. "Like Santa Claus. Or Jesus."

"I don't know, Josh."

"If she bites us, will we become zombies?"

"I don't know."

"Was Jesus a zombie?"

"What?"

"He supposedly rose from the dead, right?"

Josh was an unusually smart kid, but he sometimes followed his thoughts to inappropriate places, at inappropriate times.

"Can we save the atheism discussion for later?"

His face pinched in apparent confusion. "I'm just questioning the historicity of the gospels concerning Christ, specifically the assertions of his divinity without any corroboration outside of the canon."

From the mouths of babes. "Are you reading Richard Dawkins again?"

"I follow him on Twitter. He makes some great points."

"We're about to die, Josh. Let's stop talking about religion."

"Isn't that the best time to talk about it?"

I stared at him. "How old are you again?"

"Look, Randall, I'm just saying that maybe Jesus is real, and a zombie, and he bit a bunch of people and started an epidemic."

"So where have all the zombies been for the past two thousand years?"

He pursed his lips. "Wyoming."

This was one of our dumbest conversations, ever. But it was also keeping us from becoming hysterical with fear, so I went with it. "Wyoming?"

"It's the least populated state, but it's big, almost a hundred thousand square miles. Lots of room for zombies. Plus, it's the only state that's a rectangle. It would be easy to put a big fence around the state, keep the zombies in."

"I don't think the zombies came from Wyoming," I said.

"How do you know? Have you been to Wyoming?"

"No."

"Has anyone we know been to Wyoming?"

"What does that have to do with anything?"

"We don't have any first party proof, only hearsay, that there aren't any zombies in Wyoming. Wyoming is a thousand miles away. How did the zombies get here?"

He seemed to think about it, then said, "Uber."

"Hey," I said, turning to look at the door. "They're gone."

"Think they went back to Wyoming?"

"Maybe."

Or maybe they went in search of something to break down the door with. Did Grandma have an ax in the cabin? She probably did. Grandma used to be Fire Chief in the town of Spoonward.

That's when the high-pitched whine cut through my thoughts. A moment later a drill burrowed through the upper door panel.

I didn't think, I just reacted, pulling up the ironing board barricade, smacking it against the spinning drill bit.

The bit broke off and clinked to the cement floor. Then the drill powered off.

"You broke Grandma's drill," she said through the door. "I'm telling your mother."

"Mom's gonna be mad," Josh told me, his face solemn.

"If you tell Mom," I said to Grandma, "I'll tell her you're trying to eat us."

"Grandma is trying to eat us?" Josh said, eyes huge.

Grandma began to pound on the door again. "Let your poor grandmother in. She's starving."

"How about your pocket candy?" Josh asked her.

There was a pause. Then, "Randall ate it all."

Josh turned to me. "You ate all the candy, Randall? You a-word!"

"I didn't eat the candy, Josh."

"Smell his breath, Josh," Grandma said. "Smells like peppermints, I bet."

"Let me smell your breath, Randall."

"That's crazy!" I yelled, covering my mouth. I had eaten a peppermint a little while before Grandma had gotten attacked, and the scent might have still been on me. The last thing we needed right now was to argue.

"He took it all," Grandma said, "and when I told him to save some for his little brother, he said Josh stinks like poopy."

"I don't stink like poopy!" Josh made a mean face.

"I didn't say that, Josh. Can't you see what she's doing? Grandma is trying to turn us against each other."

"Open the door, Josh," Grandma cooed. "Then you and I will go to the market and I'll buy you a whole shopping cart full of candy, and we won't let Randall have any."

I could see Josh was considering it. I had to find a way to save us, fast, before he betrayed me and got us both killed. My eyes searched the laundry room for some sort of weapon. All I saw were laundry supplies. I didn't think fabric softener would help in this situation, much as it made my shirts smell like spring. But there, above the supply shelf, was...

A window.

It was only half-size, leading into the window well right outside the kitchen. Josh and I liked to go in there sometimes because animals like salamanders and frogs and mice often got trapped inside.

"C'mon," I told my brother, grabbing his hand. "We're getting out of here."

I told him to climb the shelf and open the window. Josh surprised me by doing it without complaint.

BOOM!

The banging had resumed. I chanced a look at the door and saw one of the three hinges had fallen off.

"Hurry up, Josh."

"Randall!" he squealed.

"What?" I stared up at him, alarmed.

"There's a mouse nest in here! It's awesome!"

"We don't have time now, little brother."

"The mouse has a bunch of babies."

"Really? Lemme see." I hurried up the shelf next to him, looking at the nest. "Awesome."

"They're pink and don't have hair yet. Got your phone?"

"Way ahead of you." I used my phone to take a picture. It probably wasn't the right time but, hey; mice babies were cool. Then the door burst inward with a giant *BANG!*

"We gotta go," I said.

"Don't step on the mice."

We climbed out of the window well, careful not to step on the mice.

"We should hide," Josh said, "wait for Mom and Dad to get home. They'll fix this."

"What if Grandma finds us?" I asked. "I think we should run."

"Where?"

"We can go to our neighbor up the road."

"It's a gravel road," Josh said, "covered with rocks and sticks."

"So?"

"Your foot is bleeding."

I looked down at my injured foot, and seeing the blood made it hurt three times as much. I seriously needed to get some shoes on. Then I remembered my flip flops were on the pier.

The pier...

The boat!

Boating would be quicker than running, and Grandma couldn't come after us if we were on the lake.

There was only one slight problem; I wasn't allowed to take the boat out by myself. I knew how to drive it, but Grandma and my parents were too worried to trust me.

"C'mon!" I said, pulling Josh's arm. We ran to the stairs leading to the dock, me limping on my tip toe so I didn't aggravate the wound. The boat was a Bass Tracker, fourteen feet long, with a 40 horsepower Mercury engine.

"But you're not supposed to—" Josh began.

"Would you rather swim?"

"No. You know I suck at swimming."

"Then this is our only option."

"How about the paddleboat?" Josh asked.

The paddleboat had two seats and pedals like a bicycle.

"The paddleboat has a top speed of a two-legged turtle," I said. "You want to risk that?"

Josh glanced worriedly back at the house, then shook his head. I carefully put on my sandals and we climbed aboard Grandma's bass boat. I told Josh to untie us while I sat in the driver's seat, reaching for the ignition.

No keys.

"Josh, you need to stay here. I have to get the keys."

His eyes widened. "Don't leave me again, Randall."

I didn't want to. Hoo boy, I really didn't want to.

But, once again, I had to.

"I'll only be thirty seconds. Go ahead and count, like we're playing hide and seek."

"I hate this idea. We should stay together."

"Count. I'll be back before you reach twenty."

Josh began to count slowly. I jumped out of the boat and hobbled up the pier, heading for Grandma's house. She always kept the keys on the kitchen table.

I got to the patio door and paused, looking through the window. The kitchen was empty. I eased the door open, slipping inside, heading for the table.

No keys.

I began searching cabinets. I didn't find keys, but I did find Grandma's stash of hard candy. I grabbed a handful, shoving them into my swimsuit pocket, pausing to eat a butterscotch. (I had to, to get the smell of peppermint out of my mouth, so Josh wouldn't think I'd been eating candy.) Then I started going through the drawers, until I found one with keys in it.

About a thousand keys.

"Jeez, Grandma. How many locks do you have?"

She must have saved every key she'd ever had, going back to the Civil War. The boat key had a yellow sponge thing on the key ring so I knew what to look for. No idea why it had that sponge thing, but I was glad it did because I found it pretty fast. Once I grabbed the key, I limped back onto the patio—

—and found the path blocked.

Grandma and Gustav.

"You're too young to take the boat out by yourself," Grandma said, wagging a finger at me. She moved closer. "Now give me the keys, and let me eat your face."

I made a move to run back into the house, but Gustav was fast, blocking my way.

"Please, Grandma. Don't do this. I love you."

"Grandma is so hungry, Randall. She needs something to eat so badly."

I tossed her the butterscotches.

"Eat these," I said.

She made no effort to catch any, and they fell onto the porch.

"I think you also have some peppermints."

Keep them talking, Randall. As long as they're answering questions, they aren't chewing on you.

"I know something sweeter than peppermints," Grandma said, smiling in a way that I didn't like.

"Chocolate?"

"Not chocolate." Grandma stepped closer to me, crunching a couple under her heel.

I began to move slowly away, to the side of the porch, watching for any signs of them pouncing.

"Cookies?" I asked.

"What I'm thinking of starts with the letter R."

"Uh… raisins?"

At this point, I was just buying time.

"You know what it is, *Rrrrrrandall.*"

Then her eyes became slits, and she growled so low it made the hair on my knuckles stand up, "I'm so terribly… terribly… HUNGRY!"

She lunged. I turned away, folding myself over the porch railing, letting gravity pull me over it, then falling face-first onto the ground a meter below. I broke the fall with my hands, rolled, got a pinecone in my mouth, and wound up in a sitting position, facing the pier.

Above me, on the porch, Grandma and Gustav peered over the railing, looking furious. I spit out the pinecone and began to run toward the lake.

Behind me, I heard the rustle of leaves and two monstrous grunts as the two elderly zombies vaulted the railing in pursuit.

I darted around some skinny pine trees and saw Josh in the boat. He was pointing at me and yelling something.

"Josh! I got the keys!"

"They're behind you!" he yelled.

No duh. I didn't need to turn around to see, because I heard them. Their growls. Their feet pounding against the earth.

Practically close enough to grab me.

I couldn't make it to Josh in time. And if I did, the zombies would get on the boat.

For some reason, I thought about this morning. Me, Dad, and Josh fishing at sunrise. I hooked one and Dad coached me as I played the fish.

"Careful, son. Don't pull too hard. Let him wear himself out."

Someone shoved my shoulder. I fell forward, skinning my knees on the dock.

"That fish is huge, Randall!" Josh said, ready with the net. "A giant bass!"

I managed to hang onto the boat key, but Grandma grabbed my hair and pulled my head back.

"We got him, Randall!" Josh lifted up the net like the bass was his, so proud even though it was just a little two pounder. I unhooked it and threw it back. "You'll be next," I said to Josh.

But he hadn't caught any fish that morning.

I wondered if he would ever have another chance.

"Randall!"

I stared at Josh, waving his arms on the boat, and realized something for the first time. We said *I love you* all the time, usually at bedtime when we said it to Mom and Dad. But until that very moment, I didn't really understand what it meant.

It meant I couldn't let the zombies get my little brother.

"Josh! Catch!"

Unable to pull away from Grandma without scalping myself, I threw the boat keys as hard as I could. My aim was good, but my self-sacrifice turned to poopy when the keys hit Josh square in the face, bounced off, and plopped into the water.

"You s-word, Randall! You hit me in the nose! You suck!"

Stupid Josh never could catch anything.

I felt teeth on my neck. But I fought as hard as I could, and watched as Grandma's uppers fell onto the pier next to me.

"Damn dentures," she cursed.

"Don't you have any Poligrip?" Gustav asked.

"I use Fixodent."

"I always carry Poligrip on me." Gustav produced a tube of the adhesive from his pocket. "You should give it a try."

As they debated the various merits of their preferred denture creams, I mourned my failure. I was going to get devoured, and so was Josh. It was going to be awful. Have you ever seen old people eat? It's gross. Now imagine them eating you.

I looked ahead to say a final goodbye to my brother, and saw him holding the fishing net, lake water dripping off it, the keys inside.

Apparently that little yellow sponge thing on the key ring made the keys float. Good thinking, somebody.

Josh held up the net, triumphant, like he'd done earlier with my bass.

"Randall! Come on!"

Grandma still had a tight grip on my hair.

"Go without me, Josh!"

Above me, the undead argument continued, becoming even stupider.

"Poligrip is zinc-free," Gustav said.

"So is Fixodent."

"Why does it matter that they're zinc-free?"

"I'm not sure. What does zinc do anyway?"

"I don't know."

I watched Josh sit in the captain's chair and put the keys in the ignition. He'd never driven the boat by himself, but he'd sat in my lap, or Dad's, and steered.

"You can do it, Josh," I said under my breath.

And he did. He started the boat, gunned the engine, and took off.

He got all of two feet away before the mooring line held him back. Josh had forgotten to unhook the stern, and the boat was still attached to the dock.

"The line!" I yelled. But he couldn't hear me with the motor on. He just revved the motor more.

"I have zinc in my Geritol," Grandma said. "So why do I want zinc-free denture adhesive? Isn't zinc good for you?"

As I listened to the inane ramblings of the geriatric undead, and watched bonehead Josh try to drag the whole pier into the lake with zero success, I realized that I wasn't ready to die yet. Not with all of this rampant stupidity around me.

"You know what the best denture cream is?" I asked, almost hysterical.

"What?" they asked in unison.

"Extra Super Distraction Pullaway," I said.

"Huh? Never heard of it."

"Me neither."

While they were distracted, I managed to pull away, only ripping out a few dozen hairs. Then I headed for the pier, starting to sprint. Screw the foot pain.

I was just ready to hop into the boat when the mooring line came free. I must have done a bad job winding it around the tie-down cleat on the pier. My bad.

The boat took off just as I leapt into the air. I missed and landed in the shallow water, my flip-flops coming off and my bad foot landing right on a sharp rock.

"AAAAAAAAAAAAAAHHHH!"

Hurt like hell.

I must have screamed loud enough for Josh to hear me, because he slowed the boat and began to turn around.

I couldn't believe it. I was actually going to live through this nightmare.

That's when Grandma yelled, "CANNONBALL!" and jumped onto my head.

For a little old lady, she hit like a linebacker. I went under, pinned to the bottom of the lake, my face in the sand and very little air in my lungs.

I wondered if drowning was better than being eaten alive. They both sounded bad. But then, there weren't many ways to die that were appealing. Smothered by swimsuit models? Getting hit in the head by a home run ball when the Cubs win the World Series?

That wouldn't be too bad. But knowing the Cubs, I had a much better chance of being smothered by swimsuit models.*

As my lungs burned and my brain screamed for oxygen, I heard a roar in the water. It grew louder and louder, until it blotted out all thoughts about girls in bikinis.

---

* This was written in the summer of 2016, before the Cubs actually won the World Series, but neither co-author has yet been smothered by swimsuit models.

Well, all girls but Jaclyn Swedberg. It was hard to stop thinking about her. My Dad had a Playboy under his bed with her pictures in it, and she was maybe the hottest babe ever.

In fact, as far as last thoughts went, thinking about Jaclyn Swedberg wasn't a bad last thought to have.

Then the roaring sound was practically on top of me, and when I realized what it was I became even more panicked.

No, Josh! Don't…!

Then there was a *THUNK!* as the boat hit Grandma. But any momentary relief I felt from being free was countered by the 40hp motor propeller spinning inches away from my face. It came so close it actually trimmed my bangs.

I swam away, narrowly avoiding a decapitation, and then popped to the surface alongside the boat, gasping for air.

"Randall!"

Josh put it in neutral, and the boat coasted into the shore—

—right next to Gustav the zombie.

I swam to the ladder next to the motor and pulled myself onto the boat, just as Gustav was climbing onto the bow.

"Josh! Reverse!"

Josh pulled the throttle back and gunned it. I fell forward, onto my hands. But so did Gustav, falling right off the boat, and into the lake next to Grandma.

And then we were zooming away from them, actually getting away, and I let out a strangled sound that was somewhere between a giggle and a sob.

"Slow down, brother," I said, patting his shoulder as we reached the middle of the lake. "You did good."

"Grandma got run over by a bass boat," he sang, to the tune of that reindeer song.

I smiled, enjoying the relief of still being alive, and shut my eyes. My breathing slowed down and the sun warmed me up. My foot was throbbing, but I felt pretty lucky.

"Uh, Randall?"

"What?" I said peeking open one of my eyes.

"Do you think they know how to swim?"

"Who?"

"Them."

Josh pointed. I stared at the shore line and I saw zombies. Elderly zombies, standing at the water's edge, watching us. Dozens of them.

Maybe even a hundred.

His Barn on Lake Niboowin
Five Hours Earlier…

The most stereotypical redneck you can imagine held a lightning rod in the palm of his three-fingered hand. How this came to occur is an interesting story (to the parties involved, which was solely him.) Each of the fingers was actually a thumb that he'd gotten fresh from a buddy who worked at the local funeral home.

"They already dead, they don't need 'em no more," Einstein reasoned, and paid the mortician a pack of smokes for each, even though the skin on one was slightly darker than his, so people always thought that finger was dirty.

Einstein would've been happy with his original set of fingers, but he'd used the band saw wrong when he tried to make an automatic beer launcher for his above ground swimming pool and decided if he had more thumbs he could get a better grip on that band saw or any other thing that looked like it needed more thumbs on it.

Like a different band saw.

Since all of his thumbs worked, Einstein felt it proper to call himself a genius; after all, he'd sewn them on himself and used steel screws to secure them to the bone and it worked. A damn fine job considering he'd done it all under the influence of Jack Daniels Tennessee Whiskey. Then he'd used fishing leeches to get the blood flowing to his new appendages, a trick he learned from the TV show *E.R.* He went through two bottles of cat antibiotics to fight off infections that damn near killed him, but the end result was something to be proud of, and obvious evidence of his superior mind.

"Look, Debs!" he bragged to his wife when the last fever broke. "If man's only advantage against other animals is a thumb, well I am triply advanced!"

"If you're so smart, how'd you cut off all your fingers in the first place?" she countered.

He told her to hush up. That showed her.

He called himself Einstein, because famous scientist Albert Einstein was the only person he knew of that had an intellect to rival his own. His real name was Rupert. Which he disliked. Especially when Debs called him that, because the way she said his name it sounded like a slang insult.

It also sounded like an insult when she called him Einstein.

Pretty much anything she called him sounded insulting.

His wife's full name was Debbie-Sue Ellie-May Bobbie-Jo Franklin-Jane. She was named after her grandmother, Grandma Franklin, and her grandfather, Grandpa Debbie.

He called her Debs for short.

Einstein would perform his genius experiments in a barn located on the east end of his wooded three acres, kitty corner to his sheet-metal house and sheet-metal bass boat which rested purdyfully near the edge of Lake Niboowin. Sheet metal was cheap and strong and shiny, up until it rusted real bad, got holes in it, and cost him a fortune to solder his house and boat back together.

So, technically, his house and boat contained more of the expensive solder than the cheap sheet-metal.

Einstein's wife never wanted no part of his "genius experiments". Whenever she used those words, she made air quotes with her fingers and rolled her eyes. She didn't like a single thing he ever invented, including the above ground swimming pool, made out of sandbags and plastic wrap. Debs called it a *stupid stagnant pit of mosquito larvae*, and questioned why they needed a pool at all when they lived on a lake.

That woman had no vision. Einstein sometimes wondered why he married her.

Oh, yeah. The big boobies.

Clevis, his bestest buddy who'd been with him since they was fetuses, always supported Einstein's experimentin'. Clevis thought Einstein was brilliant, called himself his assistant, and would often volunteer as a test subject. Though most of Einstein's genius experiments ended up as enormous, epic fails, Clevis always had the will to try another.

When he was a baby, Clevis had been dropped on an escalator, and fell for forty-six minutes before somebody thought to shut off the electricity. That might have had something to do with it.

After his automatic beer launcher failed to launch, Einstein got back to his genius experiments, intent on helping his bestest buddy. Clevis always complained that he needed to get on the roof of his barn, but he didn't have a ladder long enough to reach.

Einstein went to work to build something to help Clevis.

"Why doesn't Clevis just buy a bigger ladder?" Debs asked.

Einstein told her to hush up. That showed her.

The inside of Einstein's barn looked like a hick version of Frankenstein's laboratory. Stripped-down wires were everywhere, and cords knotted all over the walls and ceiling. Tables piled high with mechanical and laboratory stuff. An unreasonable amount of tools. His outboard motor winch with a 500 pound capacity. Lots and lots of tractor parts. A large collection of buckets, containers, and mason jars. His Corner of Shame (which he didn't like to think about 'cept when he had to). An aquarium full of leeches, which fed off of a very unhappy looking carp.

Occasionally electricity would zap in the background just like in those mad scientist labs in old movies, but instead of some cool gizmo, it was due to something shorting out or a wire frying.

"That barn is a fire hazard," Debs would nag.

He didn't bother to tell her to hush up that time. Because he was looking at her big boobies.

Einstein also had posters of guns on the walls, many of them peppered with bullet holes. He liked guns. A lot. He had a twelve gauge shotgun loaded with armor piercing slugs always at the ready in case a bear wandered in, and it was wearing body armor.

Other assorted firearms were in the house, locked in a safe so no one could steal them. There was probably some irony there, somewhere.

Einstein had been working all night for Clevis and even missed his favorite dinner—bacon and beans—which Debs claimed she made from scratch but all she really did was open a can of beans and crumble up some bacon in it.

A loud knock made Einstein crease his eyebrows and turn off his blow torch.

"Who is it?" he blurted.

"Clevis! Are ya almost done?"

The sound of Clevis's voice made him smile.

"Just about. Come on in."

The large barn door creaked. Clevis pattered over and hovered near Einstein's shoulder.

"It's like noon, Clevis. Don't ya sleep 'till one?"

"Yeah, but I'm just too darn excited! Can't wait to see what you invented for me. I need to clean all them rocks off my barn roof."

"How'd you get rocks on your barn roof?"

"I threw 'em up there," Clevis said.

Made sense.

"Alright, Clevis, you ready?"

Clevis jumped up and down and squealed like a little girl, one of his less pleasing attributes.

Einstein gave his invention a few whacks with a socket wrench. "Just a bit more… and… done!"

He stood back to take in the fruits of his genius.

It was a parachute connected to a fire canister connected to a lawn chair. When the fire canister was on, the heat would fill the parachute and lift up the passenger. In theory. The miniature prototype he'd made earlier burned like kerosene poured onto a pile of dead leaves. But that didn't take gravity into account, probably. The bigger version should work just fine.

It was sort of like a hot air balloon, just not as bulky. Those things were big and unwieldy. Einstein's flying chair could fit in the flatbed of a midsize pick-up, if you left the tailgate open.

Einstein smiled with his chin up and nodded proudly at his project. Clevis gave Einstein a bear hug.

"Thanks, partner! It's... it's a beauty."

"Well, come try it out."

They dragged the contraption outside, into a clearing that was formed by the fire caused by the prototype. Clevis got into the chair, smiling wide.

We all know what happened next. The flying chair went up about eight inches, caught on fire, and Clevis burned to death.

But even Clevis's screaming demise didn't deter Einstein. Setbacks were merely opportunities, cloaked in sadness. Einstein wasn't going to let a minor thing like death break up the bestest friends ever.

When the flames died down, Einstein dragged Clevis's smoking corpse to his workbench. His friend looked a lot like a giant piece of burnt bacon. Smelled like it, too. Which made Einstein's stomach rumble because he'd missed supper.

"Such a tragedy," he said.

But then he realized there would be leftovers, and his spirits perked up.

Clevis's death was also kind of a tragedy. At least, it would have been for an ordinary man. But for a genius, it was a challenge.

Einstein had a good think about how to bring Clevis back to life, and was considering something with leeches and tractor parts, when he heard the sound of thunder.

A storm was a'comin'. And with it, a light went on in Einstein's genius brain.

An *electric* light.

Einstein opened up the hatch in the roof of his barn with a shiny green button that had to be pressed in a specific clicking sequence that only he knew. The sky was dark and gray, the clouds already popping with lightning. A rain drop fell on the tip of Einstein's nose, and thunder rattled the walls again.

He ran back to his workbench, picked up a lightning rod made from a weather vane and lawnmower blade, and stuck it in the middle of Clevis's chest, which looked and felt a lot like a Thanksgiving turkey, still warm from the oven.

Einstein wrapped Clevis up with baling wire, and attached him to a table that lifted to the sky with a complicated block and tackle pulley system using an outboard motor as a winch. Then, in a bit of extra inspiration, he covered Clevis with leeches.

With a pull of the starter cord and a rev of the throttle, up went Clevis, the lightning rod sticking out of his chest like, well, a lightning rod.

As Einstein waited for Clevis's life to restart, he spent time with yesterday's newspaper, doing the Junior Jumble. It was a hard one, and he devoted a good twenty minutes trying to unscramble GNEUIS, to no avail. His concentration was shaken when thunder roared like an elephant just as lightning zapped the rod, making Clevis's body shake and light up even brighter than when he was on fire.

Einstein lowered his best friend down, eager to welcome him back to the land of the living.

Then sound came from Clevis's lips. But it wasn't words. It was a sizzling noise.

Clevis didn't seem any different, other than the bacon smell had gotten stronger. Einstein pressed his fingers against Clevis's neck and waited.

Five seconds passed.

Then ten.

Each passing second mocked Einstein.

He readjusted his fingers, pressing harder, and his fingers broke through Clevis's crispy throat.

This led Einstein to have what he called his *self-defeatin' thoughts.*

You're not a scientist or a genius, Einstein. You didn't even finish fourth grade. You're just a dumb redneck who thinks he's a genius, because you're too stupid to know what a real genius is. You can't even spell genius.

He was right on that last one.

Twenty seconds passed.

Why are you still checking his pulse? He's not going to come back to life. And not only that, you wasted a good six dollars' worth of leeches.

Einstein wondered if he should pick the leeches off, but they were all feeding pretty good (the ones that didn't get electrocuted by lightning), and when they got ahold of something tasty they hung on pretty tight.

Thirty seconds passed. Einstein considered CPR, decided it was too much like kissing, and settled for blowing air at Clevis's mouth without actually touching lips. But even his most heroic efforts failed to revive his friend.

Fail. Epic fail with a side dish of stupid.

Einstein slowly pulled away, the tears building up. He stared down at the floor, his heart thumping in pain.

"I'm… I'm so sorry, friend. I'm done. All done. After I cover up your death to avoid responsibility, I'm going to quit my genius experimentin'. Instead I'm going to devote my life to something else. Something worthwhile. Like a bowling league. Or watching more TV."

He threw a towel over Clevis's body and began to turn off lights in the barn. The clouds cleared up and the moon showed its lonely face. He closed up the hatch in the roof and walked, defeated, to the door.

Einstein also realized he needed to stop calling himself Einstein. Instead, he'd adopt a new, stupid name. Who was the stupidest of The Three Stooges? Shemp. From now on he'd be Shemp.

"Einstein…"

"Call me Shemp, Clevis."

"Shemp? Why?"

Shemp stopped. Had it been his imagination? Sometimes he heard voices, but he never told anyone about it because he didn't want anyone thinking he was crazy.

"Clevis? Clevis! Well slap my bottom and call me tadpole, I did it!" The genius formerly known as Shemp hurried to Clevis's table and yanked off the towel.

Clevis snatched Einstein's collar and stared him dead in the face, his eyes as white as eggshells.

"Clevis! You're alive! But your eyes…"

"Something ain't right," Clevis said. He held up his hand, staring at the burned flesh.

"You had an accident, buddy. I can… um… get you some aloe vera for that."

"It don't hurt," Clevis said.

"It don't?"

"No. I feel… heck, I feel pretty gosh darn good."

Einstein smiled. "That's great, Clevis. Lemme tell you, I was really worried there for a minute."

"I… damn! Why am I covered with leeches?" Clevis began to slap them off his body. "I hate these damn things! Oh, in my pants too! You see?"

Einstein purposefully averted his eyes so he didn't see.

"One got ahold of my giblets! Get off my manly bits, you blood-sucker! Lord, the humanity! How'd this happen, Einstein?"

"Sorry 'bout that, friend. I used the leeches when I brought you back to life."

Clevis stopped plucking leeches off of hisself long enough to give Einstein a penetrating look. "You did?"

"You were dead as a rump roast, but my genius brought you back."

"I was… dead? Wait, did the flying chair work?"

"Sorta. The design needs some tweakin'."

"Can we try it again? I really need to get up on my barn roof."

"Sure! I think my ratio of kerosene to oxygen was off. Maybe if I add some lighter fluid…"

Clevis snorted, real loud. "What's that smell?"

Einstein cleared his throat. "That's, um… that's you. You best stay away from stray dogs 'till you've had a shower."

"No, not me. It smells like fresh baked bread, apple dumplings, mashed taters with gravy—all my favorite foods rolled all up into one delicious stink."

Einstein sniffed. All he smelt was Clevis's burned flesh.

Clevis sat up suddenly.

"You should rest, Clevis." Einstein tried to push his friend back into a supine position. "You been through a lot."

But Clevis, a one-hundred-and-twenty-pound old fella who'd just been recently dead, was incredibly strong and didn't budge.

"It's you," Clevis said.

"Huh?"

"It's you who smells so good."

Clevis licked his blistery lips. Einstein took a step back.

"Look, buddy, you smell good, too. Don't get me wrong. I think it's perfectly okay for two grown men to like each other's odor. But I don't like the look in your scary eyes. What you thinkin', Clevis?"

Clevis swung his legs off the table. "We're best friends, right, Einstein?"

"Best friends," Einstein agreed.

"For a long time, right?"

"Since we was kids. You're, how old now? Sixty-five. I'm sixty-four. So more than sixty years."

"And longtime friends do things for each other, right?"

"Of course. I just let you try out my flying chair, didn't I?"

Clevis took an aggressive step toward Einstein. "I need you to do something for me, old pal."

"Name it."

Clevis smiled, his eyes getting wide. "Let me chew on your leg for a bit."

Einstein continued to back away. "That's sorta testing the bounds of friendship, Clevis."

"Please. Just one bite."

"Clevis, you know you're my oldest, bestest friend," Einstein said. "But if you try to bite me, I'm gonna shoot you right in your mullet."

"Fair enough. Debs home?"

"You can't snack on my wife none, neither. That violates all sorts of marital boundaries. What's got into you, Clevis?"

"Hunger, Einstein. Turble, turble hunger."

That's when Clevis jumped at Einstein and pinned him onto the floor, trying to bite him in the face. Clevis was strong, but Einstein had the power of genius on his side, and thinking quickly he yelled, "Look! It's Elsa Lanchester!"

Clevis had a big crush on Elsa Lanchester, back in 1955.

When Clevis turned to see Elsa, smoothing down his hair to look presentable, Einstein shoved him off and crawled for his 12 gauge. He wasn't planning on killing Clevis again. Just shooting him in the chest to slow him down.

But before Einstein could get off a shot, Clevis bolted away, through the barn door, down the path in the woods.

The path that led to Niboowin Nursing Home.

On the Lake
Present Time...

Zombies.

All along the lakeshore.

Shuffling, moaning, blood-thirsty zombies, trying to eat us. The only thing saving me and Josh from being their dinner was the water between us and them.

I'd slowed the bass boat down to an idle while figuring out where to go. We couldn't return to Grandma's house. I still had a bruise where she tried to bite me, her dentures popping out before she broke the skin. Maybe we should find some other pier, dock there, and ask some neighbor for help. Or maybe head to the boat landing, get onto the main road, and flag down a car.

But we didn't know how many zombies there were, or how far this problem had spread. Floating in the middle of the lake might be the best plan.

Josh sat at my side. His sweaty hair hung down over his eyes, and he stared at me as if I were an interesting question.

"You look like someone kicked your butt," he told me. "Twice."

I felt like it, too. Arms covered in bruises and scratches. T-shirt torn. Shorts blotted with blood. Foot still aching from the glass I'd stepped on. And I was wet, so my clothes felt like cold mouths sucking at my skin.

I was a big ball of mess.

"You don't look much better," I said. "Plus you smell."

A smile formed on his small face. "You smell worse."

"No, you do."

"You do."

"You smell like a dead fish pooping," I said.

Normally mentioning anything to do with poop would make Josh laugh hysterically. I also freely admit that poop jokes occupy a special place in my heart. But rather than giggle, my brother's face turned serious.

"Randall, are we going to die?"

Eight years old was too young to worry about death. So was fifteen, my age. But his question deserved an answer.

"What? Die? Us? No. Of course not."

"Grandma tried to eat us. So did that other old guy."

Dealing with a zombiegeddon was bad enough. When a close relative tries to take a bite out of you, it's even worse. But there was no reason to let Josh know how terrified I was.

"They're sick," I said, keeping my voice even. "They've got a disease."

"A zombie virus?"

"Maybe."

"Could be bacteria. Or a fungus. Or a prion. Prions cause bovine spongiform encephalopathy."

"Wha?"

"Mad cow disease. Infects their brains, makes them crazy."

"How do you know this stuff?"

"The Internet has more on it than just naked girls," Josh said.

"Huh. I did not know that."

"Can Grandma be cured?"

I shrugged. "I don't know. I don't even know what that SpongeBob thing is."

"Spongiform. It means sponge-like."

"SpongeBob is sponge-like."

"We're not talking about cartoons, Randall."

"We most certainly are."

I pronounced it *soitenly*, like Curly from the Three Stooges. Along with jokes about your bowels, Josh also liked slapstick. I added a *nyuk nyuk nyuk* and pretended to poke myself in the eyes, which always made him smile.

This time it didn't.

I took a big gulp of lake air. It smelled clean and outdoorsy, just like it always did. Like nothing was wrong at all.

Nothing, except for the zombies surrounding the lake.

I throttled down, slowing the boat, unsure of where to go.

"So how do you know we're not going to die?" Josh asked.

"Because I'm not ready to die. I haven't done everything I want to do."

"Like what?"

"Get my driver's license. Start sophomore year in high school."

"Get laid," Josh said.

I stared at him. "How do you know I never got laid?"

"Because you're a geek and you don't have a girlfriend."

"You're the geek. I'm more of a nerd."

"Okay, so you're a nerd and you don't have a girlfriend."

"How about you?" I said, eager to change the topic. This didn't seem like the right place to talk about my lack of success with girls. "What do you want to do?"

"I want to get my doctorate in chemical engineering at MIT and pioneer soft robotic nanotechnology."

That had been Josh's dream since he was four. Some kids are just born weird.

"That's the future," I said. "What about now? What are your short term goals? Like Dad always asks?"

Dad was big on drilling us about short term goals. It usually led to a discussion about cleaning our rooms.

Josh's face scrunched up in thought. "I want to play video games with you again."

His eyes got glassy, and his lower lip trembled. It was such a simple thing to say, but it also seemed really deep. Hope for the future, I guess. Our future.

"I want to play video games with you, too, buddy."

And then he threw his arms around me and hugged.

At that moment, time seemed to stop and I thought about how much I actually cared about Josh. He had his annoying moments, but he was a good person and I loved him and he loved me. He alone thought it was cool that the greatest accomplishment in my life was eating four large bags of Cheetos. Which, c'mon, has to be some kind of record. Four bags. They were the jumbo bags. The size of bed pillows. Each bag contained enough calories to feed a small town for a week, and I frickin' ate *four*. But no one else really recognized its importance. Only Josh. And nobody laughed harder when I told him my poop had turned orange. It hadn't really, but as I said, the poop thing really cracks him up.

"Randall!" Josh yelled above the purr of the boat's motor, his eyes so wide he looked like a cartoon.

I looked where he did. The undead had gathered on the nearest beach, less than twenty yards from my little brother and me. They shared two distinct traits; all had blood on them—from where they'd been bitten or where they'd bitten others—and all were…

Old.

Which was sort of a mean thing to say. Age discrimination was a type of bigotry, and hating others because they were different wasn't my thing.

Elderly?

Geriatric?

Retired?

In their autumn years?

Autumn. Heck, some of them were in their winter years. Even from fifty meters away, I could count more wrinkles than there were in a box of raisin bran.

For some reason, that made them scarier. I'd always thought old people were a little scary. But these zombies were terror personified. Walking along the shore, sand and mud stuck to their shins and knees. They moaned, low and deep, as if sick from some unbearable illness. Beyond the beach, within the deep woods, more appeared.

Raw, naked fear enveloped me.

Many of the women wore grandmother clothes; oversized, shapeless knee-length dresses with colorful patterns. Some were in robes. One had pink and blue hair curlers, her gown spattered with gore. There was one man in a robe, but the men seemed to prefer pajama bottoms without a top, or cargo shorts and bright polos. More than one had wrap-around sandals, with socks. But even at this distance I could see their heads jerk side-to-side in quick, deft motions, like alert birds looking for their next worm. They were old. And they were dead. But Josh and I knew, from experience, they were still very dangerous.

"They're everywhere."

No matter where I looked, there were zombies. The woods. The shore. On piers. Some had even waded into the water, heading toward us.

"The army," Josh said. "Call the army."

"I don't think you can call the army directly."

"Okay, call the Navy SEALS."

"That isn't how it works."

"Where's your phone?"

I slapped my thigh, and my phone was still in my bathing suit pocket.

My soaking wet bathing suit pocket.

I tugged it out. The case was water resistant, but the instructions indicated it shouldn't ever be submerged. I pressed the power button with my fingers crossed.

The screen came on.

My joy was short lived; like practically everywhere on Lake Niboowin, cell phone service was poor.

"No signal," I said.

I did the *no signal* dance, waving the phone around, standing on tiptoes.

"That doesn't work," Josh said. "It's not like the radio waves are missing you by three inches."

My phone chose that exact moment to ring. I stuck out my tongue at Josh—it was so rare that I was right and he was wrong—and then looked at the screen.

"You don't have your phone?" I asked.

He shook his head. "It's charging. Back at the cabin. Why?"

"Because your phone is calling me."

It rang again, and after a brief hesitation I answered.

"Hello, Randall," Grandma said. "You know you're not allowed to take my boat out by yourself."

I hung up.

"Who was it?"

"Grandma."

"Why'd you hang up? We should talk to her."

"She's not Grandma anymore, Josh. She's..."

"A zombie. I know. But we need some answers if we're going to save her."

"Save her? We need to get as far away from her as possible."

"She's our grandma, Randall. We have to try."

The phone rang again. I reluctantly answered, Josh putting his ear close so he could hear.

"So naughty of you to hang up on your dear old Grandma, Randall," she cooed.

"You're not my grandmother. Grandma would never hurt me. Not ever. Families don't do that."

"Don't act like such a naive baby. Families hurt each other all the time. When you and Josh trampled all of that mud onto my new rug, that hurt me."

"We were sorry about that. And that's not as bad as you trying to eat us."

"It's all subjective, isn't it?" Grandma said. "I didn't want mud in my cabin. And you don't want to be eaten."

"Kids these days don't do what they're told," Gustav said. "My grandparents, if they wanted to eat me, I would have obeyed, or else gotten a spanking."

"Your grandparents ate children?" Josh asked him.

"'Course not. But I'm just sayin'."

"How did you become a zombie?" Josh asked Gustav.

I was hoping he didn't say, "Jesus bit me." Not because of the religious ramification, but because I didn't want my little brother to be right.

"A zombie? I'm not a zombie."

"You're dead."

"That we shall die we know; 'tis but the time."

"What does that even mean?" I asked.

"Shakespeare," he said, using a booming, theatrical voice. "I played Brutus in summer stock, years back. I also did cartoons." He raised the pitch of his voice and said, "I wust wuv skwewy wacoons."

"I thought zombies ate brains," Josh said.

"We do," said Grandma. "But in Randall's case, that would be a very small meal."

Wow. Zombie Grandma was a jerk. And I just spent $20 of my own money buying her house slippers for her birthday.

"Randall's not all that simple-minded," Josh said. "He falls into the low end of average on the IQ bell curve, but I've met a few people who were stupider. Well, one, who's a few years younger."

"Stop defending me," I told Josh.

"Lie to them," Gustav said, loud and clear. "Tell them you're feeling better, and when they come back we'll jump them and feast!"

"We heard that," I said. "You've got it on speaker phone."

"Really? How did I do that?"

I winced at the atonal noise as Grandma pressed random keypad buttons.

"So are you both actually… dead?" Josh asked.

"I don't feel dead," Gustav said. "I mean, my heart isn't beating anymore. And I don't need to breathe, even though I do have to work the old diaphragm to be able to speak."

"But you're a zombie now."

"I don't like labels. I'm the same person I've always been, except for this insatiable hunger for human flesh."

"Did someone bite you?" Josh asked. "Was it Jesus?"

"Clevis," Gustav said. "Bit my neck."

The name sounded familiar, but I couldn't place it.

Josh grabbed the phone, "So why did you turn Grandma into a zombie? You only bit her once. You're trying to eat us, but you didn't try to eat her."

Gustav and Grandma began to giggle in a creepy, gurgly way. Like they had a secret joke they wouldn't share.

"Tell us!" Josh whined.

"There are over fifty million Americans over the age of sixty-five," Gustav said when they stopped laughing. "We outnumber our military twenty-five to one."

I took the phone back. "What does that mean?"

Josh whispered, "It means you should have called the Army."

"How about Josh?" I asked. "You were alone with him, but didn't try to eat him."

"The hunger takes a little while to kick in. And it's a fierce and terrible hunger. But don't worry… Grandma is going to make sure you never feel any sort of pain like this. Because we're going to eat… every… single… BITE!"

Josh thought we'd get some answers, but this conversation didn't seem to be doing anything other than freaking me out. I moved my thumb to end the call, but Josh quickly said, "I love you, Grandma" with all the syrupy, mushy inflection that an eight-year-old could muster.

"I love you, too, honey," Grandma cooed. "I mean, honey-roasted."

She started to cackle manically, and then my phone screen died. I tried to turn it back on, and when that didn't work I took off the case, saw that water had gotten in.

"Cell is pwned."

"What now?" Josh asked.

"Now we get as far away as possible."

I gunned the engine, pointing the bow toward the other side of the lake. The boat hit the waves head on, each one shaking us hard and making my teeth clack together. Josh had to hold onto his seat so he didn't fall off, and all the gear onboard vibrated and shifted. My brother reached out and grabbed my fishing pole before it fell over the side, but I didn't slow down. I had to get to the opposite shore, to see if it was clear.

It wasn't.

More zombies. Many more. Including several floating on inner tubes, paddling in our direction. I turned the boat around, heading east toward the public boat landing. When I got close and slowed down, I heard my little brother whimper.

"Randall! There are more that way!"

"How many freaking old people live on this lake?"

Josh met my eyes, looking unreasonably calm. "It makes sense. A vacation house on a lake is a luxury only affordable by the rich, or those who have spent a lifetime working and saving. It's a combination of pensions, IRAs, 401k plans, Social Security benefits, and smart financial retirement planning."

Josh had a genius level IQ, but that didn't make him any less of a pain in the butt.

I pushed the throttle forward, making a wide turn, heading back in the direction of Grandma's cabin. The lake was attached to a bog on the West side, shallow and filled with lily pads. If we could get there we might be able to—

WHAM!

We banged into something, the motor instantly stalling, and my chest slammed hard into the steering wheel as the boat went from full speed to coasting. I sucked in a breath and pushed away from the dashboard, looking around to see what we'd hit.

I didn't see anything. Just lake.

"Josh," I turned to him, "did you see what we just—"

Josh wasn't in his seat.

He wasn't in the boat at all.

I stood up, running to the stern, looking across the surface of the water and seeing—

Zombies. Lots of them. In the water, surrounding us.

"Josh!" I yelled.

He wasn't anywhere. I tried to look under the surface, but the lake was murky. My little brother might be only a foot away from me, but I wouldn't even see him.

Panic only took a few seconds to become sheer, overwhelming terror. I didn't think I had any adrenaline left, but my body surprised me, my heart feeling like it was being squeezed.

"Randall!"

A sound. A splashing sound.

I turned left—port—and saw Josh flailing on the surface. Right behind him, mouth open, was a—

"Zombie!" I yelled. "Behind you!"

Josh turned and looked. "There's a zombie behind me!"

"I just said that! Swim!"

Josh had never been a strong swimmer. He'd only learned last year, and his dog paddle was slightly slower than an actual dog, paddling. So the zombie—an old guy with a grizzled gray beard and a Niboowin Nursing Home nametag that read *Bob*—quickly gained on him.

"Swim, Josh! Swim faster!"

Josh continued to beat against the water, making little progress. The bearded man closed the gap.

I couldn't just stand there and watch. But what was I supposed to do? Jump in the water? Josh would cling to me in a panic, and we'd both drown. Or get bitten.

While Josh and I didn't always get along, and sometimes he was a real pain, I was more afraid for him at that moment than I'd ever been afraid of anything.

I had to save him. But how?

BANG!

A noise, behind me. I spun and saw a zombie standing next to the motor. I guessed I'd hit him with the boat. That explained why Josh had fallen out.

It also explained why the zombie's left ear was sliced almost off, hanging on the side of his face by the lobe. The propeller had severed that, and all of the dreadlocks on that same side. I assumed his hair was wrapped around the prop, which was probably why the boat had stalled.

It was also probably why he looked particularly angry.

Now what? Try to save Josh? Or save myself first so then I could save Josh?

Crazily, I remembered when Dad taught me how to drive the boat, and we'd gone over all of the safety rules again and again. Dad hadn't mentioned anything about what to do if a zombie got onboard. And he and Mom had gone for a hike hours ago, their cell phones out of range, so I couldn't ask him now.

If he was still alive to even ask.

But thinking of Dad made me recall what I needed to do when someone fell overboard.

Duh. Throw the life preserver.

We had a white ring, made of some sort of hard foam that never deflated, at the bow of the boat. I hurried to it, swinging the preserver by the nylon rope wrapped around it, then tossing it like a lasso. Josh pulled himself onto the float and used it like a kickboard.

But he still wasn't fast enough. Bob the zombie was right behind him.

I tugged on the rope, leaning back, pulling my brother closer.

"Come on, Josh!"

I took up the slack, leaned back hard, and bumped into something wet and squishy.

Knowing instantly what it was, I spun around and ducked just as the ear-dangling zombie (like Bob and Gustav, he also had a nursing home nametag that read *Deonte*) swiped at my head, barely missing me.

Then he swung his other hand, catching me right on the side of the head. He knocked me onto the floor of the boat, my ears ringing and motes fluttering in my vision. I managed to focus in time to see a large foot hovering above my face, and I quickly rolled to keep from getting stomped on. When I made it to my knees, I began to choke.

The rope to the lifesaver had tangled around my neck. Josh, in his eagerness to pull himself to safety, was strangling me.

I tried to yell for Josh, but the noose pinched off my voice and I could only wheeze. I managed to look his way, and the zombie was right at Josh's heels, trying to grip him with slimy hands.

Then the creature in the boat reached for me. I snatched up the long fishing net we used to land the big ones, and swung it hard as I could. The edge caught Deonte on the side of his head, and he staggered a few steps backward. I tugged at the nylon around my neck, untangling it, then sucked in a big breath that cleared my head.

"Randall!"

I turned again, just in time to see Bob grab my brother by the shoulder—

—and pull him off the buoy and underwater.

I didn't know what to do. Jump in after him? Throw him a life jacket? Scream in mindless fear?

I chose the screaming. Or maybe I didn't choose it. Maybe it just happened by itself.

Then Deonte lunged, bearing down on me with his full, soggy weight, pinning me to the carpet. I reached up, trying to push his chin away as his jaws snapped open and closed.

He exhaled, and a pungent odor like dead fish destroyed my nostril hairs. If I kept breathing it in, I knew I would vomit.

"You took my ear, and half my dreads, mon."

"Sorry," I wheezed.

"But you smell…" He sniffed. "So delicious. You ain't Ital, but I think I'll risk it."

I had to find a weapon.

Where was that net I just used?

I strained my biceps and chest to keep him from biting my face. Some of his sticky saliva splattered onto my cheek. I turned away, digging my chin into my shoulder, totally grossed out.

Deonte continued to chomp on the air above me. Between chomps he said, "Jah give my Livity. So… young… so… *fresh*."

His teeth got closer. My chest burned and numbed like I'd done a hundred push-ups, and I knew my strength would soon be gone.

"Leave… me… alone…." I grunted.

Deonte appeared puzzled. "What you say?" he asked, tilting his head to hear me. Except he tilted his injured side, and his dangling ear flopped in my face. It was cold, and clammy, and as it brushed across my pursed lips, under my nose, I threw up in my mouth a little.

"Speak up," the zombie said.

I knew what I had to do. But the zombie was strong, heavy, and if I used my hands he'd collapse on top of me.

There was no other choice. I had to use my mouth.

Acid burning the back of my throat, I forced open my jaws, craning up my neck to catch the wiggling ear in my teeth. It flopped back and forth, leaving a snail-like trail of slime all over my chin and cheeks. I had to use my tongue, popsicle-style, to slurp it into my mouth. Then I bit hard and thrashed my head back and forth.

His ear stretched a bit, like it was held on with a rubber band, and then it tore free and blood dribbled down on me.

The zombie's eyes got wide with surprise when he saw what was in my mouth. He raised a hand to touch the side of his head.

"That ain't irie, mon."

As his weight shifted, I got both feet up to my chest and kicked, knocking Deonte over the side of the boat with a groan and a splash.

I sat up, spat out the ear, spat again, cleared my throat, and spat once more.

The zombie sank, the ripples in the water smoothing out.

Then his hand shot up out of the water, grabbing the side of the boat. But I had the gaff in my hand; a solid, metal hook used for pulling in big fish, and I bashed his knuckles until they were as pulpy as a rotten peach and he could no longer pull himself up.

"Not irie!" he called to me as he bobbed away.

I made a mental note to Google the words *irie, Livity,* and *Ital.* Then I looked for Josh.

He hadn't surfaced yet. I couldn't even see the ripples where he'd gone under. Just the lone lifesaver, floating there.

"Josh!" I yelled, my hands cupped around my mouth to make it louder. Not that shouting would help. Even if he heard me, how was he supposed to answer while under water?

How long had he been under? Thirty seconds? A minute?

"JOSH!"

My voice echoed across the lake. On the shore, the zombies moaned louder.

I felt a sob grow in my chest, then bubble up through my lips. I didn't know what to do, and not knowing made the situation even worse.

Josh…

My little brother Josh…

I put my face in my hands and began to cry.

Niboowin Nursing Home
Four Hours Earlier...

Clevis was in awe of how big the nursing home was, and at the thought of how many cough drops were probably inside. He had a thing for cough drops since he was a child, when his mother would give him cherry cough drops, instead of attention, or love.

He liked all flavors, except for the menthol ones. That bitter hot/cold taste reminded Clevis of his father, who instead of attention, or love, would give Clevis menthol cigarettes. Clevis hated the taste, but Papa forced Clevis to smoke them, because that's what real men supposedly did. Way back then, Clevis was the only third grader in grammar school who had smoker's cough.

Which his mother gave him cough drops for.

Papa got the cancer, and the doctor removed his tongue and lower jaw. He died not long after, not from cancer, but of malnutrition, because he could only chew if he placed food on the edge of a table and pounded his upper teeth down on it. That mostly just made a mess, nutrients flying everywhere except down Papa's throat.

When Papa passed, Clevis quit smoking. He was still hooked on cough drops, though. At his house on the lake, Clevis had a secret stash that he hid from his wife, under the floorboards. Who would check the floorboards for cough drops? Who would even want to search for cough drops?

Then again, Clevis's wife tended to steal from him on a regular basis. Money from his wallet. His arthritis pain meds. The apple he was about to bite into. His car. She did this instead of giving him attention, or love.

Clevis's life was nothing if not consistent.

As he stumbled up to the front door of Niboowin Nursing Home, he gaped at its size. Ten stories high and wide as Noah's Ark, but instead of being filled with two of every animal it was filled with old folks. Folks who came from all places, like up north from the upper peninsula of Michigan, and down south from Madison and Milwaukee, and the west of Minneapolis, Minnesota, and the east of…

Well, no one from the east. The east was Lake Michigan. No one lives in a lake.

Anyway, the nursing home was big. Maybe a million residents. Or maybe it was a thousand. Clevis got those two numbers confused. But he knew he was hurt bad, and this was the nearest place to get some help. His bestest buddy Einstein (not his real name but it was how he referred to hisself) had given Clevis the honor of being the first man to try out his flying chair, and he'd been pretty badly burned over 99% of his body. The only part unburned was the skin between his toes, and between his butt cheeks.

Maybe it was more like 3%.

Each time he moved, the sound of crunching leaves filled Clevis's ears, but it wasn't even close to autumn yet. The sound was Clevis's crispy skin. Also, Clevis had leeches on him. They didn't make no sound, 'cept for maybe a real quiet slurping, but they were still pretty gross, and Clevis required medical attention. He needed skin grafts. And leech repellent. Or maybe just a good pair of pliers. Whatever would get the little suckers off.

"Ha ha ha," Clevis mumbled to himself, thinking about the leeches. "Little suckers. I'm funny."

Clevis stumbled each time he stepped, like he'd never learned how to properly walk, as he approached the nursing home through the woods. His burned skin flaked off his body, and if you shook him really hard, he would have snowed gray. He still smelled like burned bacon, and you could probably taste it in your mouth if you were near him.

But though he felt odd, Clevis wasn't in any pain. Quite the opposite actually. His sciatica, which normally flared up in the summer, didn't hurt at all. He also had a nasty ingrown toenail, one that Einstein tried and failed to remove with bolt cutters, a sack of marbles, and a disk sander, but somehow the pain from it was completely gone.

Aside from the dismay of seeing his burned skin slough off, and the knowledge that he had leeches in places where they just shouldn't be, Clevis felt pretty plucky.

Before entering the front door, Clevis considered finger combing his scorched mullet, and decided against it. He was there for emergency medical care, not to win any beauty contest. Still, it was pretty rude how the nurse working at the counter made a yuck face when she saw Clevis. She even backed away, and ran off, screaming.

How unprofessional.

Clevis looked around, drool running down his chin. There, on the counter, was half a roll of banana lemonade rhubarb vanilla cough drops. His second favorite flavor, after stanberry.

But, strangely, Clevis had no desire to pop a cough drop into his mouth.

Unless…

"Unless it's a cough drop that tastes like human flesh," he mumbled.

That was a strange thought, because Clevis had never eaten human flesh before. Earlier he'd wanted to take a bite out of his bestest buddy, Einstein. But Clevis couldn't rightly figure out why he tried to do that. Einstein never smelled particularly good, and he had a tendency to not wash on a regular basis. Plus Clevis didn't care for cannibals. True, he'd never met a cannibal before, and maybe they were nice people, but something about eating a fellow human being just seemed wrong.

Until now.

The thoughts of eating people-flavored cough drops made Clevis's stomach grumble something fierce. Or, even better, maybe he could skip the cough drops and go straight to snacking on a real live person.

Perhaps a person who was sucking on some cough drops. Best of both worlds.

The main entrance to the nursing home was just a hallway with a counter on the right side. Down the hall were two swinging doors that led to a huge living room where all the old folks gathered to watch TV, play bingo, talk about how lazy and ungrateful teenagers were, fall asleep, and engage in other old folk activities.

Clevis's Mama had been a resident here before her death from diarrhea (she'd gone on the controversial Bran and Beans Diet, and the autopsy doctor said her descending colon had exploded). Clevis had visited her here many times, even though she threw things at Clevis and called him names. The memory brought a nostalgic tear to his eye. It had been years since anyone had called Clevis *worthless* and *no good*. Other than Clevis's wife, on a daily basis.

Clevis's hunger edged him onward. His stomach got all aflutter at the thought of eating somebody. His teeth could practically feel the snap of breaking skin, which he just knew would be like biting into an apple, except people-flavored. Also, apples normally didn't scream when you ate them. Other than that, they were probably a lot alike.

He sniffed the air, smelling the delicious scent of an old man with bladder control problems.

Another sniff, and Clevis located the man, sleeping softly in a wheelchair. Clevis noticed that he had a nametag that read *Gustav*.

Strange name. Sounded foreign. Maybe he came from one of them Southern states, like New Orleans. Or Mexico.

Clevis's stomach grumbled.

Yeah, I could go for eating Mexican right about now. A big, fat burrito.

Gustav's wrinkly skin probably wouldn't be soft like a burrito. It looked chewy. Like chewing gum.

Clevis didn't care. Gum was also tasty.

People-flavored gum.

Mmmm-mmmm.

A rip of a snore came out of the old man, and Clevis shuffled forward, his mouth opening wide, a line of drool running down his chin.

Clevis knew this was messed up. Chewing on people was wrong. It was probably even in the Ten Commandments; thou shalt not eat thy neighbor. But he just couldn't stop himself. He bent over and took a big bite out of the man's neck.

Yep. Just like chewing gum.

Delicious.

The old man woke up as Clevis snacked.

"Hey! What do you think you're doing?" Gustav pressed his hand against the gaping hole in his neck.

"I'm eating you," Clevis said, still chewing.

"What? Speak up."

"I'm eating you!"

"Don't talk with your mouth full," Gustav said. "It's rude."

"Sorry," Clevis said. Skin was a lot tougher than any steak Clevis had ever eaten. But tastier. A lot tastier. "What kind of name is Gustav, anyway? Is it Mexican?"

"What? No. It's Norwegian. But I once played Pancho Villa in a community theater production of *Viva Zapata!*"

"Sounds delicious," Clevis said. He eventually swallowed and went in for another bite.

"Hold it," Gustav said, holding up his hand. "I'm not some tater tots you can just snack on. Hey! Do you got any tater tots?"

"No."

"So why'd you mention tater tots if you don't have any?" Gustav demanded.

"I didn't mention no tater tots."

"What? You got tater tots?"

Clevis generally didn't like his meals to talk back, so he tried to clamp a hand over Gustav's mouth. Gustav slapped it away.

"Stop that! What's the matter with you?"

"I'm not sure," Clevis admitted. "I've been asked that for sixty-five years."

"How old are you?"

"Sixty-five years young."

"You look like someone baked you in the oven, like a big tater tot."

Clevis shrugged. "There was a flying chair incident."

"Is that a leech on your chest?"

"And leeches." Clevis acknowledged. "Mistakes were made."

"Why do you want to eat me?"

Strangely, Clevis didn't want to eat Gustav anymore. Something about him stopped smelling delicious.

Maybe it had something to do with the fact that Gustav had lost so much blood, his heart had stopped.

"Actually, I don't."

"Then if you don't mind, I'm going to go back to my nap."

"Sorry for bothering you, Gustav."

"No harm done. Well, except for the hole in my throat. But that will heal. Or it won't. Truth told, I don't care about much since the Missus passed away. Married forty-seven years. The cancer got her. Cancer of the butt. People don't talk much about butt cancer, but it's one of the top cancers. Probably. It really gets you in the end."

Clevis didn't say anything.

"That's a joke," Gustav said. "Butt cancer. It gets you in the end."

"Funny."

"Butt cancer isn't funny, bucko. Wife had so many tumors on her bottom, she couldn't fit in her sweatpants. Say, you got any tater tots?"

"Sorry, nope."

"That's too bad. But come to think of it, I'm not really in the mood for tater tots anymore. Say, what did I taste like?"

"Salty and chewy. Lots of iron. Sort of like raw liver and tripe, soaked in blood."

Gustav nodded. "That sounds pretty good. Maybe you're onto something with this eating people idea. I never did it before, but right now it seems obvious." Gustav stood up and stretched. "How about that? Been in that wheelchair for five years, couldn't ever get up without a nurse helping. Now I feel young and spry. Like I'm sixty again. I used to be an actor, you know. Did I tell you I lost my wife to butt cancer?"

"Maybe we should split up, search for food on our own." Clevis said. He was getting tired of the butt cancer talk. It reminded him of Mama's exploding colon.

"Fine by me. Fine by me. I haven't been outside in a very long time," Gustav licked his dry lips. "Maybe I'll take a little stroll along the lake, see if there is anything to nibble on…"

Underwater
Present Time…

The zombie pulled Josh under so quickly he barely had time to suck in a breath.

He squirmed and twisted, fighting the bone-chilling water that shrouded him, trying to get free, to get those awful, slimy hands off his shoulders. But the monster was too strong, and soon its arms were around Josh's neck, drawing him closer, pulling the boy against its clammy body.

Drowning was bad. Zombies were even badder. Josh couldn't imagine how this situation could get any worse.

Then he felt teeth nibbling at his ear.

Josh screamed, precious air bubbling up around him, and he thrashed with a full scale freak-out, the fear giving him the strength to pull away.

The zombie let go, presumably floating to the surface.

Josh did not.

Josh's eyes clamped shut as his small frame sank into the murky depths of the lake. The harder he thrashed against the water, the deeper he went. His heart pounded so loud he could hear it, and even with a genius brain like his, he didn't know what to do. During Josh's first swimming lesson, a skinny teenager named Kyle had tried to teach him to hold his breath face-first in the water without pinching his nose. Which was impossible. Josh had practiced for a whole hour with limited success, and then the first lesson was over and he had to move onto the second lesson without mastering the first. Every lesson had been like that, and eventually, after swallowing half the pool, he'd kinda learned a limited, ineffectual doggy paddle.

But the doggy paddle didn't work *underwater.*

Josh's feet hit the mucky bottom of the lake, and panic squeezed him. It was like stepping into cold pudding, mixed with slimy weeds that slithered over his calves.

Josh kicked hard as he could, and he had to mash his lips shut to keep from inhaling. The hair on his head swished around like it was spaghetti in space, and he flailed his arms, insane to get to the surface to breathe, but he wasn't getting anywhere.

Where's Randall? Why isn't my big brother saving me?

He continued to kick and paw at the cold water, his arms over his head like he was reaching for the sky.

Then something grabbed his tiny wrist.

Randall! To the rescue!

He almost blew the air out of his lungs in joy, but an odd sensation stopped him.

Since when did Randall's hands get so slimy?

Josh squinted through the murk, saw the piercing eyes, the open mouth drawing closer.

That's not Randall!!!

Josh was tugged out of the weeds, and he felt those awful teeth press against his arm.

The young boy didn't think. He reacted.

Josh pulled his knees up and kicked off of the living dead creature's chest, hard as he could push. That was the momentum he needed to send him upward. It wasn't a moment too soon, either, because his lungs felt like two burning paper bags, and his brain was starting to go dark.

Josh kicked like a frog and took big handfuls of water, pulling himself through the water.

Almost there...

Just a few more feet...

And then, like the answer to a prayer, Josh could see the sun through the lake's surface. It was the most beautiful thing ever. Josh could practically taste the air.

Closer...

Closer...

SPLASH!

Josh finally broke the surface, and he inhaled so fast and hard that he got water in his mouth. This prompted a coughing fit. It wasn't easy to cough and swim at the same time, and Josh swallowed more of the lake as he began to sink again.

"Josh!"

Randall was calling, but Josh didn't see him. He began to twist in the water, trying to keep his head high with a frantic dog paddle, searching for the boat.

There! His big brother! Randall was finally going to save him!

"Rand—"

—and something grabbed Josh's ankle and tugged him under again.

This time, rather than panic, Josh felt a strange calm come over him. No matter what he did, he wasn't fast enough to get away.

Now that he accepted that, he had to explore his other options. And there was only one that made sense.

Fight back.

But how? This creature was more than twice his size. Josh needed a weapon, but he didn't have one. Randall was allowed to carry a pocket knife, but Dad said Josh was still too young for one, so all he could keep on him was nail clippers.

What was he supposed to do, give the zombie a manicure?

For some reason, thinking of manicures made Josh remember a Three Stooges short called *Slaphappy Sleuths*, where the trio ran a gas station and part of their customer service included giving patrons manicures. It was a ridiculous thing to think of at a time like this, unless...

Unless Josh's freakishly large brain was trying to tell him something.

What was the connection? What was the…

The idea hit Josh with eureka-type clarity. But for it to work, he had to get closer. Josh forced himself to relax. He opened his eyes, staring at the creature trying to eat him.

You want to do this?

Certainly!

But in his head, Josh pronounced it soitenly, like Randall's bad Curly impression from earlier. Then Josh did a Three Stooges eye poke, making a V with his fingers and jabbing them hard into the zombie's peepers.

Apparently the undead didn't like their eyes being poked any more than the living did, because the zombie immediately let go.

But Josh wasn't through. He went for the nose pull and twist—a Stooge classic—tugging hard.

Oh… that's just nasty…

Josh remembered the baby game called *got your nose*, when a grownup would pretend to steal a kid's nose after tugging on it.

Well, Josh did the same thing. Except he actually pulled off the old zombie's nose. He tried to shake it off, but his finger got wedged in one of the nostrils. It hung there like a fleshy onion ring, twirling around without coming off.

Then—*won't it ever stop?*—something grabbed Josh again.

But this time, he was yanked to the surface. Josh looked up, saw the dark shadow of the boat, his brother leaning over the bow and pulling him in.

Josh broke the surface, inhaling big then coughing up water. His ears were clogged. His head ached. His whole body shuddered with chills.

But he was alive.

Randall quickly pulled him into the boat, then wrapped Josh in a towel.

"You okay, little buddy?"

Josh nodded, shivering. Randall hugged him, and it was just about the best feeling ever.

"I… I got you something, Randall."

Smiling, Josh held up his hand. The zombie's nose was speared on it, like a big, fleshy ring.

"Oh… that's just nasty," Randall said.

"I picked it just for you." Josh grinned even wider. "Get it? I picked the nose!"

Randall made a face. "That's totally disgusting. Throw it away."

Josh was too giddy with being alive to listen. He made a sniffing sound, holding up the nose like a puppet. "Dude, you smell something?"

Randall slapped the nose away, and it went overboard. Almost immediately, a fish came up and swallowed it whole.

"I think we've been using the wrong bait," Josh said between giggles. Then he stood up, stepping on something squishy.

"What's *that*?"

"A zombie got in the boat. It's his ear."

"Well," Josh said, looking at his shoe. "I guess he heard me coming."

Josh's giggling soon become full-body sobs, and Randall hugged him until he calmed down.

"I… I was so scared…" Josh stammered.

"Me, too."

"I think I'm hysterical. Or in shock."

"You'll be okay. I need you to get it together, buddy."

"I almost died."

"We're not out of this yet. Look around."

Josh didn't want to. He knew what he'd see.

But he did. He looked. And it was worse than he could have guessed.

More zombies on the beach. More zombies in the water. Some of them only a few yards from the boat and closing in fast. A whole army of old, dead people, with angry faces and mean eyes.

Coming to eat them.

"Randall… we need to go."

"Motor won't start. I had to paddle over to you with the emergency oar, and it took forever." His shoulders slumped. "We can't get away."

"You checked everything?"

Randall nodded.

"Even all the tricks Dad taught us about the motor? Working the choke and priming it by squeezing the fuel bulb?"

"I tried. That zombie's long hair practically destroyed the propeller."

Josh's nose scrunched.

"So what are we supposed to do?"

Randall shrugged, and Josh saw he couldn't look him in the eyes anymore. His older brother stared across the lake, his face pinching.

Randall was usually a lot stronger than Josh, both physically and mentally. But the way he stood at the moment, and the way he acted, he seemed weak.

Really weak.

Josh didn't feel protected by him like he normally did. Instead, Josh felt a responsibility to protect his older brother. It was a weird feeling, but he knew Randall had been doing the same for Josh his whole life. Looking past all the wedgies and wet willies, Randall always made sure Josh was loved and protected.

Now Josh needed to return the favor. He felt cold and tired, but determined.

"Where's the emergency oar?" he asked Randall.

His brother pointed to it, floating away. "I dropped it when I pulled you in. I'd row us out to it, but…"

Randall shrugged.

From the lake, one of the zombies caterwauled with what sounded like hunger.

Josh took inventory of the boat. His eyes passed over several fishing poles, and two large tackle boxes filled with vintage lures. They also contained pliers, stringers, knives, and first aid kits. There was a net, some life jackets, some bottled water, bug spray… Josh considered turning the aerosol insect spray into a flamethrower, but there weren't any matches on board.

The waves notched up a bit, pushing them closer to the opposite shoreline. Josh stared at a lonely pier to the east of them. It was aluminum, and small, but looked solid. No zombies were near it, so it was a good place to dock.

If they could get to it, they could leave the boat and try to find Mom and Dad. How to get there was the golden question.

Josh was never swimming again, no way, not for the rest of his life. Even with a life jacket on, he was *not* getting in the water. Maybe Randall could swim over there, but then what? There were some nylon mooring lines on the stern and bow, but they were only a few feet long. The rope on the anchor was thirty feet. But the pier had to be fifty yards away.

He looked around the boat again, trying to come up with a plan. Wrapped in the towel to protect himself from the wind, Josh squatted next to a lure box and opened the clasp and lid. He stared at Dad's Musky Prowlers: antique baits his father had gotten on eBay for $90 each. Randall and Josh weren't allowed to fish with the Prowlers because they were too expensive to replace. The boomerang-shaped lures were huge, seven inches long and almost two ounces, with heavy duty treble hooks and through-wire construction. Dad had joked that he could cast up into a tree with one of his musky poles and swing from it, the lure and line were so strong.

Strong enough to swing from. And the heavy lures could cast the length of a football field.

"Randall!" Josh said, excited by his idea. "Let's use the Musky Prowlers!"

"Now isn't the time to fish, Josh. And Dad will kill us if we lose one."

"We're going to get killed anyway, butthead, if we don't do something. See the pier?" Josh pointed to it.

"Too far away."

"We use the musky poles, catch the pier, and reel the boat over to it. The poles and line are strong enough, and the Prowler is so heavy it will cast like a rock."

Randall stared at Josh, hope blossoming on his face. "That could work. That could really work!"

They scooped up their musky poles and attached two of Dad's Prowlers to the fifty pound leader wires.

"Wind is against us," Randall said. "Adjust your magnetic brake."

"I will."

Casting into the wind with a baitcast reel ran the risk of a backlash. They called it a *bird's nest.* When the reel spun faster than the line went out, it became a huge, tangled mess which could only be fixed by cutting all the line off and restringing the spool, or spending forever working out the dozens of knots with a toothpick.

They didn't have time for either. Zombies were within ten yards of the boat and swimming in fast.

Josh adjusted his grip on the fishing pole, leaned back, and flung the lure with a perfect rainbow cast, sailing toward the pier—

—and coming up short. Very short.

He reeled in fast as he could, but the big lure wiggled and vibrated deep into the water, causing a lot of drag. Pulling in the Prowler was harder than pulling in many of the smaller fish they'd caught that trip. Though Dad allowed Josh to fish for muskellunge—the world record musky was caught in this same county in Wisconsin, weighing in at more than sixty-nine pounds—it was a very hard fish to catch. Not only were muskies elusive (they were called *the fish of 10,000 casts* because that's how many it took to get a bite), but they were tough fighters. As badly as Josh longed to catch one, sixty-nine pounds was more than he weighed and he didn't want to be pulled overboard, so he hadn't done much musky fishing.

It was hard work.

Randall, on the other hand, loved to musky fish. And his first cast seemed right on the money, heading straight for the pier, before the wind blew it off course by a few feet.

"You can do this, Randall," Josh said, still fighting with his lure. "It's too far for me, but you can do it."

Randall reeled in fast, beating Josh's bait back to the boat, and then cast again.

ZIP!

PLOP!

Miss.

Josh's hands and arms began to cramp, but he kept reeling, and kept encouraging his sibling. "C'mon, Randall. It's all up to you. Save us. Save us, big brother."

The zombies had gotten closer. Josh bit back a whimper when he saw one only a few yards away. It was missing a nose. And it didn't seem happy about it.

"I can do this," Randall said quietly, eyes laser-focused on the pier.

Randall leaned back.

Then he let it rip.

The lure soared.

Hung in the air. Hung for so long it looked like it just stuck there, like some chewing gum thrown against a window.

Then—

CLANG!

The lure hit the pier and skittered over the edge.

Randall reeled in, and his rod bent.

"Got it! I got it, Josh!"

At that same moment, Josh's pole bent nearly in half. He thought he'd hit a weed, but then there was a giant tug on his line. A tug that dragged his lure under the water and shook it.

It was a fish!

A *huge* fish!

"Randall! I got one!"

Randall didn't turn to look. He was obviously concentrating on reeling in, on pulling them toward the pier.

"What do I do, Randall?"

As hard as it was to hold on, and as beaten-up and tired as Josh was, the thrill of catching a fish energized him. Especially a musky. And this one was gigantic.

"Just drop the pole, Josh."

"It's a musky! And Dad's Prowler! I can't drop it!"

Josh's whole body shook with effort, his arms and legs straining. He could barely reel in.

Then the strain on the line let up, and Josh knew what was happening.

"It's going to jump, Randall!"

It breached the surface, as Josh expected.

But it wasn't a musky.

It was an elderly woman. Zombified. Her housedress recognizable even though the lake had washed out the bloodstains.

Josh's eyes grew twice their size, and his bladder clenched. He couldn't breathe. Couldn't talk. But somehow, the words still escaped his lips as he stared at the monster holding the lure in its hands.

"Grandma?"

CLEVIS

Niboowin Nursing Home

It was a frustrating exercise in frustrating frustration.

The geezers all smelled good. Some like cheesecake. Some like biscuits and gravy. Some like a ham sandwich on rye with a side of slaw. And the first bite tasted good as it smelled. But after swallowing a mouthful, it always soured in Clevis's mouth, and he couldn't bring himself to take another nibble.

Which was the triple frustrating part, because the turble hunger in his gut did not let up.

So he went room-by-room, hour-after-hour, greeting the residents a friendly howdy-do, chatting a bit about mundane things, tearing a hunk out of them with his teeth, then moving on.

It sorta reminded Clevis of a heart-shaped box of chocolate candy, the fancy kind that had always had a paper-wrapped assortment of nougats and caramels and truffles and those bitter jelly ones no one liked. To avoid the jelly ones, Clevis would take a tiny little bite of each chocolate, to check what flavor it was.

Except in the nursing home, everyone tasted like one of those awful jelly candies. And to make it quadruple frustrating (a frustrating exercise in frustrating frustration that frustrated him), by the time Clevis got to the second floor, he had competition. Some of the people he bit earlier had begun roamin' around, looking for snacks. It became like Double Coupon Seniors Night at *Paco Chang's All You Can Eat Chinese Mexican Buffet.* Way too much competition. Clevis wasn't that fond of the burrito fu yung to begin with, and he didn't want to have to wait in line for it.

And even worse than the long lines were the people endlessly complaining about the long lines, which Clevis complained about every chance he got.

There had to be tastier food elsewhere.

So Clevis left the Niboowin Nursing Home and wandered out into the woods to find some better eats, without no crowds of complainers.

He followed his nose. Since the flying chair/resurrection incident back at Einstein's laboratory, Clevis's sniffer had become powerful as a bloodhound's. He tracked down a dead squirrel that smelled like blueberry muffins but tasted like dead squirrel. He found some wild rhubarb that tasted like wild rhubarb. He located a deer that smelled like pepperoni pizza but it outsmarted him by being faster than he was.

And then Clevis smelled the most delicious smell he ever smelled. Better than anything at the nursing home. Better, even, than a whole box of cough drops.

Drool dribbling down his chin, Clevis ran toward the smell as fast as his elderly legs could carry him.

JOSH AND RANDALL'S PARENTS

Somewhere in the Woods…

Barbara's feet were screaming at her.

She wished she'd worn thicker socks. The serene walk in the woods she'd planned with her husband had turned into an endurance test:

Sticks and weeds and nettles cutting her legs? Check.

Rocky, sloped terrain, with no trails to speak of, that caused her ankles to ache and swell? Check.

Mosquitos and biting flies, buzzing and stinging? Check that one, too.

She'd worn her new hiking boots to break them in, but instead they were breaking her feet, the leather interior rubbing her toes to raw blisters, the non-existent arch supports giving her cramps.

So much for a pleasant stroll.

Each step became increasingly difficult, sweaty, itchy, and painful, and Barbara hated herself for ever leaving the house in the first place. She and Tom hadn't found a nice, romantic spot to open the wine and sandwiches they'd brought along, and the backpack strap felt like it had dug a permanent dent into her shoulder. The bug spray was empty. It seemed like they'd been traveling much longer than the two hours they'd been gone.

But this walk had gone beyond discomfort and irritation.

Something in Barbara's stomach told her the forest didn't want them there.

Maybe it was the way the trees strained out more and more sunlight the further they walked. Or how the branches seemed to curl and snarl, growing ever thicker. Their sunny, bright morning had somehow become a dark, gloomy trek to find their way back home.

Barbara shivered. Though she'd been vacationing in Wisconsin since she was a little girl, Barbara had never gotten used to the woods. She remembered being ten years old, playing tag in the trees with Judith, her older sister. Barbara had thought she'd tripped over a branch, and into some thick mud.

Then the stench hit.

It wasn't a branch.

Barbara had tripped over a dead deer. A dead, decomposing deer, half eaten, its insides jellied and swimming with wiggly maggots.

The image was bad enough, the source of a thousand nightmares. But the odor of rot and decay, so thick she could taste it in the back of her throat, was something that would never leave her. She screamed so hard because the smell was so awful, and in screaming Barbara had emptied her lungs so she had to take another huge gulp of putrid air to scream once more. She kept that up until she vomited and passed out.

It took her years before she dared venture into the woods again.

Sure, the forest looked pretty. It was full of life, and for the most part smelled wonderful. But even though she'd since grown up and gotten over childish fears, a small part of Barbara knew the beauty was just a veneer. A mask. Beneath it was something ugly and terrible.

There was death in the woods, everywhere you looked.

Each summer, Barbara dutifully visited her mother up at the cabin. Her boys, Josh and Randall, loved it. Her husband, Tom, loved it.

Barbara tried to love it. She made every effort to. But fishing with her family made her ache for the poor fish being caught. Driving up and down the winding country roads never failed to showcase a deer that had been run over, its insides smeared across the asphalt like a giant, congealed plate of spaghetti. And even the simplest walk through the woods would always reveal the bones of some poor creature, some bird or chipmunk or snake, and the rotten smell that went with it.

So far, this terrible hike had been death-free. But it was only a matter of time. Barbara could feel it. As if the death that the woods kept hidden was waiting for her, ready to jump out and scream, "Boo!"

She wasn't sure how much longer she could hold herself together before panicking.

"Are you sure this is the right way?" she asked Tom, for the tenth time that hour.

Her husband, whose legs were even more scratched and bruised than Barbara's because he'd been clearing brush ahead of them, cast a quick glance back at her, his face somewhere between frustration and hopelessness.

He didn't answer. He wouldn't admit what Barbara dreaded; that they were lost.

They kept walking.

The woods became darker.

"Tom," she whispered to him, "I think we're going the wrong way."

Barbara hoped he would say something reassuring.

He stayed silent. Stoic Tom, trying to prove some macho point.

"Tom, can we please just go back? This just doesn't feel right." Barbara was closer to Tom now, gripping on his arm.

"You always do this," he said, the irritation apparent in his voice.

Barbara bit her lower lip. She felt like she'd been tolerant for hours. She deserved a medal, not his criticism.

"I want to go back."

"Okay."

"Now, Tom."

"You're welcome to lead the way," he said, making a sweeping arm gesture.

She marched ahead of him, under dead branches, over big rocks, going right a couple paces, going left. Then Barbara pulled out her phone from her shorts, and held it high above her head, doing the 'try to find a signal' wave.

"My phone isn't working. Let me have yours."

"Mine won't work either. We have the same model phone, and the same carrier."

"Let me try it."

Tom handed over his cell phone like it was the hardest task he'd ever had to complete.

No signal on his, either.

Barbara felt an inner rage start in her chest, then burst from her mouth.

"Dammit, Tom! We should have turned back earlier. We're lost and this place is freaking me the hell out!"

"Don't blame this on me. You're the one who wanted to find a picnic spot."

"We passed a dozen picnic spots!"

"We didn't pass any."

"How about that fallen tree?"

"It was filled with ants, Barbara."

"That clearing, an hour ago?"

"Poison ivy."

"That big rock, not far from Mother's house."

He made a frowny face. "Actually, that big rock would have been a good spot."

Barbara was about to scold him for not stopping at that lovely big rock, but then she heard something in the woods.

The sound of something moving.

Barbara pulled closer to her husband. His red shirt clung to his sweaty back, and she breathed in his scent, grateful for it. Grateful it wasn't—

Barbara gagged, a lump forming in her throat.

She smelled something.

Something that wasn't her husband.

Something *awful.*

Barbara clutched Tom's shoulder, pulling him to a stop.

"Do you smell that?"

He sighed, overdoing it. "It's the woods, Barb. Things die in the woods. You gotta get over this phobia. If it's dead, it can't hurt you. If you want to worry about something, worry about bears. Or drunk hunters. Not some dead raccoon."

Barbara cleaved herself to Tom, her arms locking across his chest. "Do you see a dead raccoon?"

"I don't see anything."

"Are we lost?"

"No. We can't be. There's a road that goes around Lake Niboowin. We haven't hit it. So we must be circling the water."

"So where are we?"

"I think we're on the east side of the lake." He looked around. "Near the nursing home."

Barbara buried her nose in her husband's hair, wanting to smell him instead of the rotting odor. As she did, she gagged and pushed away.

"Tom! You stink!"

He turned around, wrinkling his nose. "That's not me. I smell it too. Wow, that's disgusting."

Barbara held her breath. Somewhere, in the woods, a branch snapped.

When she breathed again, the smell had gotten worse.

Tom coughed. "Man, it's like overcooked bacon, gone bad."

Barbara reached for his hands, held them tight as she could. "It's getting stronger, Tom."

The stench was coating the back of her dry throat. She dug her nose into her shirt, but could still smell it through the fabric. Her tummy tightened, starting to spasm.

"Probably a breeze carrying it in," Tom said.

"Do you feel a breeze, Tom?"

"No. But the smell is getting worse. And it's obviously something dead. So it has to be a breeze, or— "

"Or what?"

Tom grinned, eyes wide. "Or we're being stalked by some kind of undead forest animal."

She frowned. "That's not funny."

"A zombie deer?" He snapped his fingers. "ZomBambi! Stalking through the woods, seeking out the hunter who killed his mother." Tom put his hands next to his head so they looked like antlers from an eight point buck.

Barbara could usually tolerate Tom's teasing, and even enjoyed it to a degree, but she was miserable and the smell was freaking her out.

"Stop it, Tommy."

His grin deepened, and he spoke in his Boris Karloff voice, "They're coming to get you, Barbara."

"Stop it. You're acting like a child."

"They're coming for you. Look!" Tom pointed. "There's one of them now!"

Barbara couldn't help herself. She looked.

There was nothing but empty forest.

Her eyes darted everywhere, trying to spot movement in her surroundings. The rotting aroma increased, a sour and disgusting smell that made her want to hurl. She could feel her heart slamming really hard at her ribcage.

Barbara wanted out of the forest. Right. Now.

Then she felt teeth graze her neck.

She screamed, above the sound of her husband's laughter, and she took off into the woods, part of her knowing that Tom had just given her a tiny nip to scare her, but that was the adrenaline hit she needed for her fight or flight reflex to take over.

"Barbara! I'm sorry!" he called after her, laughing.

It felt good to run. Even though twigs swatted her face and nettles nipped her legs, Barbara was primed to sprint a marathon at a record speed.

"It was a joke, Barbara! Don't run away! You'll get lost!"

His voice was a long echo through the thick underbrush.

Her legs pumped even faster, two pistons that would never run out of energy. Then she tripped over a rock and went tumbling, face-first into the forest bed, skinning her elbows and knees, kicking up dead leaves and mud.

"Barbara!"

Tom's voice sounded far, and she couldn't pinpoint which direction it came from. Barbara frantically viewed her surroundings, heart pounding in her ears. Every direction looked the same, nothing could distinguish itself. Just monotonous, thick, brown trees that stretched as far as Barbara could see.

"Tom!"

He didn't answer.

"TOOOOOOOOOM!" she held the word until her breath gave out, then prayed for a response.

She waited.

And waited.

Then…

Barbara thought she heard him yell, but couldn't be sure. It didn't sound like he was calling her name.

It sounded like he was screaming in fear.

"TOM!"

Was that jerk playing another joke?

Barbara stood up, her legs no longer feeling like pistons. Instead, they felt like they no longer had any bones in them.

Ahead of her, about forty yards, she spotted a figure.

"Tom!"

Barbara took a shaky step forward, then stopped.

Tom had been wearing a red shirt.

Whatever she was looking at was all brown.

A deer? A bear?

Barbara couldn't tell who or what it was, but it seemed to be moving closer to her. She could hear its footsteps crunching on the leaves.

What the hell is that?

It didn't walk like a person. It was unsteady, staggering in a zigzag.

Fear spiked through her. She recalled a self-defense class she took, years ago, that said you should always trust your fear. It was your subconscious sensing danger.

She took the car keys out of her pocket, and gripped them tight with the pointed ends poking out of her fist. Something she also learned in that class. A punch to the face could stun an attacker. A punch to the face with keys could blind him.

Barb steadied herself, watching as the thing came closer. Then the smell slapped her in the face.

It was that same rotting scent as before.

"Tom!" Barbara called again.

Tom didn't answer. And Barbara was sure that brown thing wasn't Tom. In fact, her gut told her that thing was the source of the stench. It reeked of rancid, burned meat, which got stronger as it came closer.

Some sort of animal that had gotten burned?

Barbara felt her pulse quicken, the need to flee strong. She might be getting herself even more lost, putting more distance between her and Tom, but the primal revulsion she felt was growing so fast that she had to run.

Then the brown thing made a sound.

A very human sound.

It sounded like, "Help me."

Barbara stood still. She stared, rooted to the spot.

"Help me," it said again. Its voice was deep. Male.

"Who… who are you?" she said, her voice high and squeaky.

The man stumbled closer, the smell becoming overpowering. Barbara's eyes began to water. She held her nose and blinked away tears.

"I… was at… the home…" the man said, getting to within ten yards. Barb now saw that he was burned. Badly burned.

Still, she couldn't bring herself to go to him. Her legs seemed paralyzed.

"Were you in the forest fire a few days ago?"

"Blood…" he croaked. "So much blood… Help me…"

"I don't have a cell phone signal. I can't help. Unless… do you know the way out of the woods?"

"I need… help… so many people… so old…"

He continued to close the gap between them. Barbara felt her gorge rise. Not only was the smell worse than that dead, rotten deer from her childhood days, but this man was so horribly burned he shouldn't have even been alive, let alone able to walk.

"Help me."

"What do you want me to do?"

He stopped a few feet in front of her. He was too horrible to stare at, but Barbara couldn't turn away.

"I tried them… I tried them all…" he rasped. "But after a single bite, they stopped tasting good."

He licked what was left of his burned lips, his tongue the color of spoiled liver.

"Wha… what do you want?"

"Help an old man out," he said. "You smell delicious. Like a big, juicy, blood-filled cough drop."

Then the brown thing lunged at her, mouth open wide.

Still in the Boat…

OK, Randall, you can do this.

You're fifteen. Practically an adult.

Just focus.

Focusing wasn't easy. There were at least a dozen elderly zombies in the water around us, getting closer. I was cold and tired and hurt. The last few hours had burned some horrible memories into my mind, things I'd never forget if I lived to a hundred.

A hundred? I wasn't even sure I'd see sixteen…

Focus!

Breathe in.

Breathe out.

The line was taut, my pole bent to near breaking, the Heddon Prowler hooked on the pier twenty yards away. I had to just keep slowly reeling in, no jerky motions, and it would pull us to the dock, and then we'd be off of the Lake of the Living Dead.

Don't snap the line. Don't pull the lure free. Slow and steady wins the race. I'll be the big brother that Josh needs. I'll show him, myself, and the world that I can do this.

I'm not the loser I think I am.

I sighted down my line to my lure, keeping full attention on it to correct for the slightest sway of the boat. The waves were taking us east, the pier was to the north, so I had to keep turning my body so my rod tip pointed at the target. I reeled in slowly, half a revolution a second, my thumb and index finger tight on the reel handle, my fist practically glued to the butt of the pole.

My feet pressed against the seat in front of me, so I could use my thighs to hold myself steady while reeling in. Kind of like how kayakers row. My baitcaster had a 7:1:1 ratio, meaning that a full three-sixty crank would pull in about two-and-a-half-feet of line. And this was musky line, fifty pound test, strong enough to hang from.

Inch by agonizing inch, I pulled us closer to the pier. Away from the swimming zombies. To safety.

I actually began to think we were going to make it.

Then the wind kicked up. Cold wind that raised goose bumps under my damp clothes. And with the wind…

Waves.

My pole bent further, the line stretching with a *PING!* sound. My muscles tensed and I braced my legs.

The boat rocked. I had no choice. I had to let out some line before it snapped or tore the lure off the pier. I flipped the switch on my reel and began to crank backward, relieving some of the tension. My damp clothes, and the sweat on my face, chilled me all over. My hands began to cramp. I bunched my shoulders, continuing to let line out. The pier getting farther and farther away. I ignored Josh as he yelled and carried on about some fish he caught. I think he said it was a musky, but I had 99% of my attention focused on saving us. A musky was a nice fish, tough to catch, but he should have been worried about other things.

Focus, Randall, our lives are on the line.

No pun intended.

Well, maybe a little of the pun was intended…

"Bro! Help me!" Josh stood up in the boat as he fought the fish.

"I'm kinda busy here!"

The boat continued to drift east and the wind got fiercer, whipping hair across my eyes. The line continued to creep out of the reel, and my lure had become too far away to see. I checked my reel.

There wasn't much line left.

"Randall! I... saaa... maa!"

Josh's voice was high and squeaky, practically a scream. It was impossible to understand him when he yelled like that. He sounded like a dolphin.

But it sort of sounded like he said he saw Grandma.

Last we'd seen Grandma, she was in the lake somewhere, zombified and hungry and eager to spend time with us in a way that wasn't mutual. Fewer things can ruin a child's relationship with a relative than cannibalism.

My spool was nearly empty, I took my chance. Flipping the switch back, I tightened the star drag and fought against Mother Nature, holding on with all I had. The boat yawed, pulling me forward.

The line was too tight. There was no give.

I'm going to drop the pole.

I hit the release before Josh and I were dumped overboard. The boat immediately rocked back, throwing Josh into the tackle box.

The one we forgot to close...

It burst open, antique lures and fishing tackle exploding outward like a fireworks fountain, my brother getting rained on by artificial baits.

I watched the pole fly out of his hands, shooting like an arrow into the water, and he began to yell as dozens of hooks stuck into him.

"Randall!"

I had to help him.

I shoved my fishing rod into the wedge of the seat, and it stuck there like a giant antennae. Zombies were all around us, their paddling getting ever closer, groaning and gurgling and snapping their jaws.

"Stay still!" I told my struggling brother.

He went rigid, lures caught in his clothes and hair, hooks glinting, looking like a Christmas tree in a Hellraiser movie.

A lump big as an apple formed in my throat. I'd gotten a hook in me before, in my arm, and once those barbs pierce the skin they were impossible to rip out. Dad had to use pliers to push the hook out the other side, then snip off the barb. It was an awful experience. And Josh had dozens of hooks all over him.

"I'm freaking out, bro."

His voice did sound like he was freaking out.

"Me, too." I blew out a hard breath and tried to stay calm. "You need to stay still or the hooks will go in deeper."

Josh stood as stiff as a statue as the boat swayed in the waves. His arms were stretched out before him, Frankenstein-style. I started pulling all of the loose lures off of him, ones where the barbs weren't stuck, and dropped them into the open tackle box.

"The zombies are getting closer," he said, eyes darting back and forth.

I carefully pulled two Arbogast lures off his shorts. He had a Creek Chub Injured Minnow stuck in front, in the worst possible place a man could get hooked.

"Josh… you feel anything in your… uh… in the bathing suit area?"

"Huh?"

He carefully lowered his head—careful because of the lures in his hair—and the bit of color still in his face drained out.

"Awwwww… no… not there…"

"Just stay still."

I reached for the lure, a slight tremor in my hand.

"Be careful, Randall. I'm going to need that when I get older."

"What?" I asked. "Your Injured Minnow lure?"

"Just be careful or I'll have two injured minnows!"

I hesitated, not wanting to grab my brother anywhere near his junk. His shaking didn't make things any easier.

"Stay still."

"I am. You're the one shaking."

"This is a delicate procedure here."

"Just do it, before I pee myself."

I gripped the bait, firmly, and gave it a tentative tug upward.

The cloth on his shorts stretched out, the barb staying embedded.

"Is it… uh… are you hooked?" I asked.

"I don't think so."

"Okay. I'm going to tug really fast. You ready?"

He nodded. I took in a deep, slow breath and yanked.

The lure tore free, without catching any skin.

"Randall! Your pole!"

I glanced over my shoulder. My pole was coming loose from the chair.

If I lost the pole, we couldn't get to the pier.

I reached for it—

—missed—

—and the rod plopped into the lake.

Foolishly, I tried to bend over the bow after it, and a zombie splashed up out of the water and grabbed my shirt. A real ugly one, who looked a lot like my high school principal. All bald and age-spotted with curly, gray hair coming out of his ears.

I slapped him away, falling backward as my shirt collar ripped, tripping over the open lure box and landing hard on my butt.

"It's getting in the boat!" Josh cried. He was tugging at the lures in his hair, his eyes so big he almost looked like a cartoon.

I got to my feet, scooped up the lure box, and threw it at the zombie as he swung his leg over the port side. He fell back into the water, along with around a zillion dollars' worth of Dad's baits.

I turned back to Josh, who'd managed to free his hair of hooks, but still had at least a dozen on his shirt.

"Stop moving, Josh! I'm going to cut your shirt off."

He nodded, looking as frightened as I felt, and I found a small pen knife on the steering dashboard and began to slice a ragged zig-zag through his wet tee. When I cut all the way through I slowly peeled the shirt off his body, taking all the lures with it.

"Ow! Randall!"

Okay, all except one. It stuck in Josh's chest, above his right nipple. A Heddon Moss Boss, with a really big hook.

And the hook was in deep.

Josh winced at it. "That's not good."

I touched it, softly, and he yelped. I pulled away.

"You should leave it there," I said. "Makes you look tough."

His lower lip began to quiver. "Get it out."

"I don't think I can push this through. You want me to pull it?"

Josh nodded, squeezing his eyes shut.

"On three," I said, grasping the Moss Boss tight. "One…"

I yanked up hard as I could. Josh's skin stretched out, really far, and he howled. When his skin couldn't stretch anymore—and, really, it looked like a pink teepee about three inches long—I gave the hook a sharp twist and it came free.

Josh began to cry.

Then a zombie hand grabbed the side of the boat.

Then another.

And another.

I looked at Josh, his mouth turned down in a long sob.

I didn't know what to do next. But for some reason, rather than panic, I felt a weird calm take over.

"You okay?" I asked Josh.

He opened his arms and hugged me.

"Sorry it hurt so bad, little bro."

"They're everywhere!" he said, shivering in my arms.

I held him tighter.

"It's gonna be okay."

But it wasn't gonna be okay.

I didn't know what was worse; getting eaten by zombies, or letting my brother down.

I was a loser. A giant loser.

I wasn't the big brother Josh deserved.

"Look, it's not all bad," I said, stretching for something positive in this tornado of awful. "I know you lost your pole, but at least you hooked a musky."

He pulled away and looked up at me. "That wasn't a musky."

I frowned, "What was it, then?"

The bow of the boat tipped down, and a skinny arm hinged itself over the edge. It was followed by a head. A familiar head. A head that read us countless bedtime stories, baked us thousands of cookies, and kissed countless boo boos.

"Did you miss me, boys?" Grandma said. Then she cackled like a witch.

Lost in the Woods...

Tom opened his eyes and stared up at the forest canopy.

He was on his back. In the woods. The last thing he remembered was—

Tom bolted into a sitting position. He rubbed the back of his head, found a tender knot. Some crazy old man wandering through the woods had knocked him over. Tom must have hit his head, blacked out. He took a quick look around. The man was gone. So was Barbara, Tom's wife.

He stood up, leaning against a tree to steady himself.

"Barb! Barbara!"

The forest didn't answer.

He checked his cell. Still no service. Mosquitoes buzzed in his face, dive bombing and retreating before he could swat them. Night was coming. Being out in the woods, after dark, wasn't on Tom's bucket list. He wanted to find his wife, to get back to the cabin. Do something mundane, like fish. Play a board game. Talk to the kids about their day. Drink a beer.

Instead, Tom and Barbara had gotten lost and separated, and Tom had gotten assaulted.

This wasn't how summer vacations were usually spent. And this was all his fault.

Tom chewed the inside of his cheek while surveying the trees. He forgot what color clothes Barbara had been wearing. Hopefully not green or brown.

"Bar-bar-aaaaa!"

He listened, trying to hear past the whipping wind and flapping leaves.

"Bar-bar-aaaaa!"

After almost half a minute of no response, he practically had to swallow his heart back down. He had no compass, but he could make out the sun setting in the east. He knew they were still near the lake, and assumed they were on the south side.

Before he left, Tom made an X mark on a tree with a stone. He headed north.

Walking.

Stopping.

Calling.

Waiting.

Making another X. Not as good as a trail of breadcrumbs, but at least he'd know he wasn't going in circles.

Tom continued the cycle, getting more frustrated with each passing minute. Was Barbara lost? Was she safe?

Had that man who'd attacked him gotten her?

She'd run off, frightened, because Tom had been teasing her. He'd just been playing around. Trying to lighten the mood since the hike had been so shitty. But the thought that he might have scared her into the clutches of some backwoods psycho...

Tom rested his hands on top his head, sucked a deep breath, and forced himself to not punch a tree.

"Bar-bar-aaaaa!" Tom's voice cracked.

"Tom!"

It was faint, but not far. Tom couldn't pinpoint the direction.

"Baby? Where are you? Keep talking!"

"Help me!"

"Where are you?"

"Help!"

"Honey? Are you okay?"

"Please! Stop!"

Stop? Why would she tell Tom to stop?

Unless…

Unless she's not talking to me.

"Bar-bar-aaaaa!"

"Stop it! Oh God stop it!"

Tom sprinted. "I'm coming, Barb!"

"Tom! Hurry! He's— "

He? Who? The guy who'd knocked out Tom?

What was he doing? Hurting her? Raping her?

Killing her?

"He's EATING ME!"

Trees blurred past Tom and he tried to look everywhere at once, calling his wife's name, trying to find her in the endless maze of leaves and trees and branches and—

He caught something moving in his peripheral vision, and skidded on his heels to a stop.

Something blue.

Blue! Barbara had been wearing her light blue shirt and jeans!

But she hadn't been wearing any red. And there was a lot of red.

Oh… no…

Tom weaved his way through the trees, dropping to his knees next to her, instantly soaking his pants in his wife's blood.

Barbara was clutching her tummy, moaning. Shock had drained most of Barb's healthy color away. Her breaths came out in sharp gasps, and she was staring off into nothing.

He touched her face and she screamed, her arms flailing out.

Tom cradled her head in his lap. "It's me, honey, it's me."

Her thrashing stopped, and her eyes found his.

"Oh, Tom…"

"Where are you hurt, Barb?" he said, daring to examine her.

"My side. He attacked me."

"A man?"

"An old man. Smelled like burned meat. He grabbed me and I fell, and then he started biting…"

Tom looked away from his wife, searching the forest, hoping the man was nearby because Tom was ready to tear his head off.

He was nowhere to be found.

"Where'd he go?"

"I punched him, Tom. I punched him with the car keys. They stuck in his back, and he ran away."

Tom returned his full attention to the mother of his children. She was strong, a fighter, and it was one of the reasons he loved her so much.

"It hurts, Tom." She was pressing a hand to her stomach.

"Let me see, babe."

Hands shaking, he lifted her bloody shirt. Dirt and leaves stuck to her belly, around and in the jagged bite wounds. Blood continued to ooze out, and Tom's head suddenly felt heavy. He looked around for the backpack she'd been carrying, found it a few yards away, and scrambled over to it. He removed some of their picnic items—a bottle of wine, some apples, a bag of cubed cheddar—and located the first aid kit he always packed for *what if* scenarios. Opening the plastic container, he found a few Band-Aids, a roll of gauze, some iodine wipes, an ACE bandage, and various packets of pills. No butterfly strips or sutures that could close the wound, and not enough iodine to disinfect a paper cut.

What a sad, shitty first aid kit.

"The wine," his wife said, pointing.

It was a cheap wine with a screw off top, which Tom had off in seconds. He wasn't sure the alcohol content was high enough to sterilize her wound, but at least it would clean off the dirt. Tom began to pour it on Barb's belly, and she voiced her displeasure and held out her hand.

"Let me *drink* it, Tom."

"Oh. Yeah."

He handed her the bottle, and opened up a package of Tylenol tablets, which she took between gulps.

"I'm going to wrap up the wound best I can," he told her. "You'll need to sit up."

She nodded, and Tom helped her into the right position and did his best with his limited supplies.

"I always made fun of you for carrying around that stupid kit," Barbara said, offering a grim smile.

"It *is* a stupid kit."

"It's better than wrapping me up in dead leaves and twigs. Check if you can get a signal."

He almost protested—there was no way they'd get a cell signal in these woods—but went through the motions to appease her. His eyes widened when he saw his cell phone.

One bar! He had one bar!

Tom considered calling for help, but he guessed any rescue attempt would take hours before it arrived, if it could even find them. Instead, he quickly brought up an app.

"Is it working? Call 911!"

"I'm checking Google Maps. If I can find our location I can get us back home."

"We need to call for help, Tom!"

"Barb, first we need to know where we—"

Barbara reached for the phone, knocking it out of Tom's hands.

He grabbed for it on the ground, missing and knocking it away, stretching for it and snatching it up—

—and the signal was gone.

Tom waved the phone around, desperately trying to locate the hotspot again.

"Is it gone?" His wife's voice was cracking. "Tommy, is it gone?"

Tom felt like screaming. He squeezed his eyes shut and hugged his wife as she took the phone from him.

"I'm sorry," she said. "I didn't… Tom! Google Maps loaded! It found our location."

Tom looked at the screen. They were less than a mile away from Grandma's cabin, and only a hundred yards away from the lake. If they could make it to the water, following the shoreline back to the house would be simple.

"Can you walk?" he asked.

Barbara nodded, her breathing labored.

"Alright, up you go."

She swung her arm around him, and Tom took her weight on his shoulders and upper back. He kissed her cheek and some color came back to her face, like a flower blossoming.

"I love you," Tom said.

"I love you, too."

"Agree to never hike again?"

"Agreed."

He got his bearings, checked the sun through the canopy, located west, checked the map on the phone, and then began to take her toward the lake.

"Wait!" she protested. "The wine!"

They went back for the bottle, each took a long sip, and got on their way.

Still on the Boat…

"Grandma?" I said, voice cracking.

Josh's musky Prowler lure was clutched in her hand, the big treble hooks poking through her fingers like the world's scariest jewelry.

My mind couldn't grasp that this monster was my grandmother. The caring, gentle woman I'd grown up loving so much had become a creature out of a horror movie; one who eyeballed me like she was jonesing for seafood and I was a steaming lobster. Her face split into a terrible grin, and a plaque-covered tongue swirled around her blue lips, as if she could already taste me.

How awful was that?

At the bow, Josh seemed mortified. He dropped his fishing pole like it had given him an electric shock, and then scurried behind me, hiding.

We both edged backward as Grandma tried to board. She snagging an ankle onto the frame, but the fiberglass proved too slippery. Her scowl deepened, and she did a chin up on the boat's side, stretching her hooked hand toward us.

"Help your poor Grandma, boys. I'm so cold. And *so hungry*."

That wasn't going to happen.

While Grandma continued to try and board the bass boat—unassisted by us—I scanned the water and counted zombies.

I stopped counting at ten. Some were so close that their hands were coming up over the sides. I saw the one who looked like my principal hang on the port side and waggle his tongue out, like a starving dog begging for treats.

"Umph!" Something—a zombie bite?—stung my ribs. I spun, but it was only Josh, jabbing me with a knuckle to keep from getting squished into the captain's dash.

We shrank back against the steering wheel as undead hands stretched out at us from all directions.

Before I went totally insane from fear, I had an optimistic thought.

"They can't get in the boat," I said.

"Why not?"

"Think about it. What do we do when we're water skiing?"

"It's too hard to pull ourselves up…"

"Right."

He snapped, his whole face brightening. "So we use the ladder!"

"Yeah, dude!"

Josh released me from his grip and ran around the boat with glee.

"How you like the water, you old farts!"

He raised his hands above his head and broke down some funky dance moves. The cabbage patch. The running man. The Egyptian. Then he broke out into air guitar, finished a quick solo, and for an encore gave all the swimming zombies the finger.

The finger wasn't a dance move. Or if it was, it would likely be banned in schools for obscenity reasons.

Josh then commenced with the mocking.

"You can't eat me! You can't eat me! Pffftttt! Lame zombies! Awhhh. Look. That poor hungry old dead man just can't pull himself on board. And we're trapped up here, two defenseless, delicious young boys…"

While I'd been enjoying Josh's victory celebration, something about his last few words made me scrunch up my eyebrows. Not the delicious comment—though that was a pretty weird thing to say. But the part about pulling himself on board.

Because, in all the excitement, I'd forgotten that earlier, a zombie *had* gotten on board. Which should have been impossible, unless he'd used…

"The ladder," I said, spinning to look at the stern—

—watching as Grandma climbed up the aluminum water-skiing ladder.

Made sense she knew about it. After all, it was her boat.

"Bite me!" Josh was yelling at the water and thrusting his little hips. "Bite my big—"

"Josh!" I warned.

Josh turned, noticed Grandma, and squeaked like a mouse that had been stepped on.

"Bite you? That sounds like a wonderful idea." She cackled again.

I backed away, arms spread out to protect Josh, wondering what we were going to do.

She held up her palm, the Musky Prowler hanging from it.

"Look what you naughty boys did to poor Grandma."

Her arthritic hands curled into claws, and she began to tug on the hooks in her palm. I winced as her skin stretched out so far it looked made of rubber.

The barb didn't pull out. Instead it split right through her flesh, leaving a long tear. But, surprisingly, there was very little blood.

"Shame on you bad boys. Now come give Grandma a kiss to make it better."

She took a step toward us. I had no idea how to stop her. So I just yelled, "Grandma! Stop!"

And she did.

Okay, Randall. Build on that.

"Grandma. I know…" I tried to push back the fear, to remind myself that she was my grandmother. "I know you're in there, Grandma. Somewhere beneath that monster you've become… is still that person we love. That person who reads us stories when she tucks us into bed. Who bought Josh a new goldfish when the old one died."

"Goldie died?" Josh said.

I snapped at him. "You're a genius, Josh. You think he could change colors from gold to silver?"

"I thought it had to do with the pH of the water."

I turned back to Grandma. "Grandma, you can fight it. I know you can. I demand you come out. You're stronger than this."

Her eyes softened. She was listening to me. My lovely Grandma was still in there, somewhere. Her rigid claws relaxed into open palms. The deep creases between her eyebrows disappeared. A mean snarl turned into a concerned frown.

"Randall?"

"Grandma?"

Could she really be back?

"I'm so sorry. My Randall." She shuffled closer. Sniffling. Whimpering. "My poor baby. What has gotten into me?"

"Grandma? Are you okay?" Josh asked.

I held my little brother back. But at the same time, I wanted her to be okay so badly that I found myself believing it.

"I've been behaving terribly," Grandma said. "You boys look so scared. My goodness, what would my Barbara think of me?"

Grandma sniffled. A tear streamed down the side of her nose. She took another step toward us.

"Stay back," I said, my voice cracking.

"Please forgive me, boys. My beautiful boys."

Her face had gone from demonic to regretful. But she still continued to shuffle forward.

"Grandma," I said. "Please don't come any closer." But my fear was quickly being replaced by hope, and guilt.

"A kiss." She mumbled, "I just want a kiss. A kiss always makes things better, doesn't it? Just a little peck on the cheek. Please."

Maybe all she truly needed was a kiss. What could a little peck on the cheek hurt? Josh did that to me all the time.

"Just…" Grandma was only a few steps away. "…one?"

"Are you sure this is a good idea?" Josh whispered.

"Maybe she's okay," I whispered back.

"She's drooling."

"That could be lake water."

I felt Josh's hand press against my back. "What if she tried to… hurt us?"

"I'm taller and stronger," I said. "I can stop her. If she's okay, maybe all the other old people are okay. She could… I dunno… talk to them. Make them leave us alone."

"I hope so. I really hope so."

Grandma stood before me and stopped. I wasn't going to lean forward, but I didn't stop her leaning into me. I slowly put my hands on her cold, damp shoulders, ready to push her away, but at the same time I tilted my cheek out for a quick kiss.

"Such a good boy. My sweet, sweet Randall."

Then her mouth opened so wide I could see down her throat.

Then she lunged like a snapping turtle.

I stretched my face away from her gnashing teeth. Her hands came up under and pushed away my wrists with surprising speed and strength.

Then came the bite.

Her teeth met my jaw and squeezed, the flesh pinching. I thrust out my arms, getting under her chin, trying to force her head back.

"Kiss your grandma!" she shrieked, spittle flying into my eyes.

The boat pitched and I almost lost my footing.

"They're climbing up the ladder!" Josh yelled.

Grandma took advantage of my imbalance and drew closer to my face. My muscles couldn't hold her back much longer.

"Josh! Help me!"

He scooted around me and yanked on Grandma's dress. Then Josh yelled through his teeth, "I thought you said you were stronger!"

Though my trips to the gym weren't always prolific, I was young and healthy and in reasonably good shape. Grandma was short, over seventy, and weighed less than I did. But even with Josh's help, her open mouth was about to close around my nose.

"Hungry!" she snarled. "So hungry!"

She tilted her head sideways and her teeth clenched over my nose. I tried to pull back but this time her dentures didn't pop out.

Then came the chewing.

Pain almost blinded me, and I shoved my left hand in her face and twisted my hips, pulling instead of pushing, using her weight against her.

Grandma slipped past, my nose popping free, and I gave her a shove overboard, back into the zombie lake.

I touched my nose then checked my fingers, looking for blood. I didn't find any; only Grandma-drool.

"Am I okay?" I asked Josh.

"Sometimes," he answered. "Mostly you're below average."

"My nose, you dork. Did she break the skin?"

Josh scrutinized me. "No. But dude, think about a better zit medication. It's like a whole galaxy of blackheads."

The boat rocked. Josh and I took frantic looks around.

The undead had completely surrounded us.

Knowing what I had to do, I opened up the storage compartment in the middle of the boat.

It was exactly what I needed.

Or more what Josh needed.

A life jacket.

I yelled for him to put it on, but I couldn't hear my own words above the pounding of my heart. When he didn't react I just stuffed it over his head and buckled it on.

"No, Randall! I'm not going back in the lake!"

"Yes you are!"

"I'm never swimming again! Ever!"

"Josh! Please!"

Behind us, a zombie stepped off the ladder and onto the boat.

"Randall, I—"

I pushed bonehead into the water, hard enough that he tumbled over all of the flailing zombies.

Then I dove in after them, undead hands grasping at me as I sailed through the air.

The cold water shocked me, and I came up behind my screaming little brother and caught a hand in his strap, kicking behind him fast as I could, using him like a paddleboard.

We headed toward the pier at a good clip, getting distance between us and the horde.

"I hate the water!" Josh coughed, his hair plastered down over his eyes.

"Would you rather be eaten?"

"Yes!"

"Want me to leave you here?"

"No! But I want out of this lake!"

"Working on it, little buddy."

"It's freezing! My balls are the size of BBs!"

"They were always that size."

Josh continued to whine so I focused on the pier. It was only twenty yards away, and we were moving at a pretty good speed.

We're going to make it. We're actually going to—

Then something grabbed my ankle.

I yelped, trying to pull away, and felt a sharp sting.

I wasn't grabbed. I was caught.

"Why did we stop?" Josh moaned.

I took a deep breath and went under. I couldn't see through the murky water so I used my hands, tracing down my leg to the source of the pain.

A line was wrapped around my ankle.

I tried to get my fingers underneath, but it was too tight. After a few moments of struggling, I broke the surface.

"What's wrong?" Josh's eyes bulged out.

"Fishing line," I gasped. "Around my leg."

"I dropped my pole. Is it mine?"

I'd dropped my pole, too, so Josh might not have been the culprit. But before I could exonerate him, the fishing line tightened and we were slowly pulled away from the shore.

Toward the boat.

I looked back, and saw Grandma at the helm, pulling in the line wrapped around my ankle. She'd picked up Josh's Prowler lure and was now tugging us in, hand over hand, as a flotilla of elderly zombies began dog-paddling our way.

EINSTEIN

Back at His Barn…

The old redneck's mouth curled into a gap-toothed grin as he plugged in the welding torch.

He didn't wear a face shield because that was for losers who cared about their safety. Besides, the bright blue light only hurt if you stared at it for more than a second or two.

After joining the components he shut off the gas and stood up to marvel at his newly crafted invention. It perched on his workbench, all shiny and glinty and ready to be tested out. This bit of genius was to correct the mishap that had befallen his bestest-friend, Clevis, who been fried the color and texture of original recipe KFC, without the alluring smell of those eleven herbs and spices. Wouldn't have been too bad—Clevis hadn't really complained—but his affliction had coincided with a desire to eat people.

That was… awkward. And probably illegal.

So, Einstein intended to fix what he started. It was who he was. That's why when he accidently cut off his fingers, he replaced them with thumbs. That's why when the 'lectricity went out while he was hungry, he invented the *Meat Stick Flashlight*; allowing him to see in the dark while providing a tasty snack. It was a triple win, because a few hours later his turds would light up the inside of the toilet bowl like a jack o'lantern.

Or better, like a *Poop o'lantern.*

Einstein yawned in the cool dusk air, and rubbed the gray hair on his beer belly. Looking around, he noticed his barn was a bit disorganized. Besides the cool stuff—like the peg board filled with tools he created (his favorite was the boomerang hammer, for pounding nails around corners), or the thick power lines that intertwined like a bowl of noodles hanging from the ceiling next to the block and tackle chain and pulleys—boxes of junk covered half the floor space in the barn, and the other half of the floor was covered in junk that wasn't in boxes.

It was a giant pain in his glowing brown backside to work in such messy conditions, but searching for the right doodad was also part of the fun. While making his latest, he pocketed twelve pennies, a Susan B. Anthony dollar, and a cool pocket knife he found as a kid when he threw a magnet on a string into the lake to see if he could catch the elusive iron crappie. He hadn't caught any iron crappie. Maybe because they were too elusive. Or maybe because they didn't exist. But the pocket knife was cool, even if it was too rusty to use, and when he cut himself on it he had to get twelve tetanus shots in the stomach. Twelve painful shots, with a needle the size of a drinking straw.

Still, finding it was proof that luck was on his side, and his newest, bestest invention was destined to work.

But what should he name this beast? Something this awesome deserved an awesome name.

How about… the *Ass Kicking Helldriver Boomstick*?

Truly an awesome name, but Einstein had already used that on another invention he made that picked wildflowers.

The *Warmonger Flesh-Smasher*?

Also awesome. Also already used, for a miniature popcorn popper (it popped one kernel at a time, for when you weren't very hungry.)

The *Cannibal Destroyer 9000*?

That wasn't bad. Though he wasn't trying to destroy Clevis, just turn him non-cannibal. But the *Cannibal Convert Back To Normal 9000* didn't sound as slick.

He decided on the TCD9 for short.

He'd scientifically modified his double barrel twelve gauge shotgun, except this didn't shoot out slugs or birdshot. It zapped out electricity. Sorta. At the end of the barrel were four defibrillator pads with springs on one side and spikes on the other. The first trigger launched them. The second sent the juice.

Problems to look out for were the lengthy charging time and the lethality, because Einstein hooked up a motorcycle battery to the stock for power. It should work, because he spent all day on it, and he didn't want to think the day was wasted. If it didn't work, it could also load twelve-gauge shells. Hopefully it wouldn't come down to that.

He craved to add one final touch: Spray painted flames on the barrel, and mastodon tusks on the sides. Einstein had a lot of dead mastodon skeletons on his property for some reason. Probably because a bunch of them died there.

He'd already put yellow glitter on the stock. Einstein had some sparkly glue sticks he got when Merl's Sparkly Glue Stick Store had their going out of business sale (who coulda predicted that?) But before Einstein finished decorating the TCD9, he had to test it out.

THUMP THUMP THUMP!

Someone was at the door.

"Yap?"

The barn door creaked open and it was his wife, Debs. Just about as old as Einstein, but still had kickin' boobs. She knew not to come in when Einstein was working, so it must've been important.

"What is it?" Einstein said, slipping into the agitated tone that he called his *married voice*.

"Well, Rupert…"

That name… His real name… It was worse than a kick in the sack.

"Don't call me that. And can't you see I'm busy?"

"Just wanted to let you know—say, what ya workin' on?"

Einstein chewed his inner cheek. As much as he still had the hots for her, she annoyed the hell outta him. The way she was able to talk and breathe.

So irritating.

"It's for Clevis," he said.

"What does that good-fer-nuthin' need a shotgun for? Ain't he got one?"

"It ain't a shotgun. It's a TCD9000."

"Looks like you just put glitter on your shotgun."

"It's more complicated than that. You wouldn't understand."

"What does the 9000 stand for?"

"Huh?"

"Did you make eight-thousand nine hundred and ninety-nine others, and none of them worked? That why you call this one the 9000?"

"It's science, Debs. You saying you want to talk science with me?"

"I'm saying you probably named it 9000 because you thought it sounded cool, and that's the only reason."

She was right, but Einstein would die before admitting it. "Just tell me what's on your mind, Debs."

"Only tellin' ya I'm visiting my mother at the nursing home. Today is her birthday."

"That so?"

"Happens every year I believe."

He checked his watch, which wasn't working, and then checked the barn clock. "Ain't it kinda late?"

"It's her birthday all day. Visiting hours until ten. You'd know that if you came to visit her sometimes."

"All those old people give me the creeps."

"Fine, then. Sit here and play Barbie make-up girl with your glitter sticks and firearms. Want me to tell Ma anything from you?"

"Yeah, tell her I'm sorry she had sex with your father."

Einstein didn't actually say that, only thunk it. Instead he said, "Tell that sweet lady I wish her the greatest of happy birthdays. We get her anything?"

"I made cookies."

"What kind?"

"Chocolate chip."

"How many?"

"Three dozen."

"Gimme one."

"They're for Ma."

"What is your Ma gonna do with three dozen cookies?"

"Eat them. That's what you do with cookies."

"Your Ma is a hundred years old," he grumped. "She eats like a bird. Two bites and she's full."

"You're exaggerating. And she's only ninety-seven."

"At least let me try one."

"You can lick the bowl. It's still in the sink. Just dump out the soapy water."

Debs left, slamming the door. He didn't care. Her cookies were lousy anyway. And to ram that point home he shouted, "I don't even want your lousy cookies!" Even though he did.

Annoyed, Einstein picked up the TDC9 and pressed the stock into his shoulder. He turned on the defibrillator, and waited for the whirring sound to stop building.

But it didn't. The noise kept increasing, getting louder and more chaotic, humming like a lawnmower with a stuck carb. When sparks began to ping off the barrels, Einstein aimed at the barn door ten feet away.

His sweaty finger pulled the trigger.

BOOSH!

The pads spewed out like an opening hand. Which was how it was supposed to work, but then all four bounced off the wood and vibrated on the floor like they were having a seizure. Wary to press the second trigger because of the potential danger, curiosity got the better of him and Einstein did it anyway.

The pads carbonized in a puff of smoke that smelled like ass. Worse than ass.

Einstein's TCD9 should have been named the *Smelly Ass 9000*.

The SA9 was now as useless as his wife's cooking. And his wife's cooking was the worst. She once made a bread spread out of bananas, vinegar, and cod liver oil. She called it *banannaise*, and it was so ineffective as a foodstuff that Einstein smeared it around his barn to keep away rodents and flies.

He smacked the SA9 on top the workbench, displeased with the results, and became nearly paralyzed with self-defeatin' thoughts.

Einstein? I should change my name to Bozo McScrew-up. Or Screw-up McBozo. Or Stupid McStupidpants.

After a redneck minute of wallowing in the pity pool, he got over hisself, then sat down, chin in hand, and tried to analyze what went wrong. The more he thought, the more his hands rubbed his face. They moved to his ear, and he plucked out a long hair the length of a new pencil.

Thinking was really hard.

After pondering for what seemed like half an eternity, he fired up his pneumatic angle grinder to distract himself from his self defeatin' thoughts, and spent a half hour making an anvil. Or rather, more accurately, making a smaller anvil out of his large anvil. Why buy a small one when you could get a large one and grind it down to the size you needed?

Einstein worked on it until his grinding wheel broke. He considered making another grinding wheel, but to do that he needed a grinding wheel. And a smaller anvil.

Life just didn't want him to win.

So he went back to thinking about the SA9. He was thinking so hard he strained himself and passed gas.

Gah! Curse his sixty-four year old intestines.

The smell wouldn't go away, and Einstein tried to recall what he'd eaten earlier that caused such stench. He remembered when he saw the greenish-brown glow.

Oh, yeah. Meat stick flashlight.

Didn't smell as bad as the SA9, though.

Einstein closed his eyes, straining his genius brain. But try as he might, he couldn't focus. A break, or a nap, was needed. Or maybe some thought-provoking television show. He wondered if monster trucks were on now.

Then the barn door opened.

"Yeah?" Einstein turned to see who it was: Clevis, hoping to be de-cannibalized? Debs, bringing back cookies because her mother couldn't eat all three dozen? That irritating state archaeologist guy, whining because Einstein wouldn't share his mastodon bones?

Someone stumbled inside, tripping and landing face-first into the floor. The person moaned, then began to squirm like a worm covered in salt. It took a moment because her clothes were all muddy, but Einstein realized it was his wife.

"Debs? You bring some cookies back?"

She continued to writhe, and Einstein found himself getting sort of unsettled.

"You okay?"

More moaning. Was she hurt? She couldn't be, because she was wiggling something fierce. The last time Einstein had seen his wife jerk around so much was that time she'd sat on a beehive, when he'd been experimenting with making his own honey in the sofa.

"Debs? You get into the bees again?"

She flipped over onto her back in a sudden, jerky move. Foam oozed out her mouth, and her eyes rolled to the back of her head.

Rabies? Was it rabies?

He looked for bite marks.

There! On her neck!

"Sneezin' Jesus with the hay fever!"

Einstein couldn't believe it.

He was a single man!

"Yeeeeee-hawwww!"

No time for celebration. He had to dig his wife a proper grave. As much as he didn't like Debs, he married her for a reason… which he couldn't remember… but, he knew that Debs hated doctors and would refuse all medical treatment, so she was as good as six feet under. And it was his legal job as her husband to bury her.

Six feet seemed really deep, though. Three feet would probably be just fine.

Two feet, even.

Or he could just drag her outside and pile some garbage on top of her.

"Debs, I'm going to look around the property for a proper resting place for you. There anything I can do to… uh… make your last moments more comfortable?"

"Hungry…" she croaked.

"You want some grub?"

He was tempted to tell her there was a bowl of cookie batter in the sink, all she needed to do was dump out the soapy water, but that seemed spiteful considering it was her last few moments on this Earth. So Einstein looked around his messy barn for some food, eyes locking on something on his workbench.

"How about an onion?" he asked, picking it up. "I can wipe the bugs off." He gave it a sniff. "Nevermind. It's a horse apple."

He tossed it aside, wondering why he had a horse apple on his workbench, especially since there weren't any horses nearby, and then noticed his wife had stopped all of her groaning and flailing and mouth foaming.

"Debs?"

She was still as a church on Tuesday. Not even her chest—which still looked pretty darn good—was moving. He crouched next to her, and felt her wrist, checking for a pulse.

Nothing.

He tried her neck next.

Nothing.

There was also no pulse in her boobs, and he checked several times.

He frowned. As much as Einstein idealized being single, this was still a sad moment for the redneck. A death in the family, no matter how well-deserved, was something to mourn. He smoothed the hair off her forehead, reverent-like. Einstein didn't want to get the rabies, but he thought it respectful to give her one final kiss. As long as he obeyed the five second rule, and didn't use his tongue, he should be able to avoid catching anything. Probably.

"Debs… you were the love of my life for about three months. The rest of the years not so much. And while I can't say there is a lot I'll miss about you, because you weren't a nice person, I gotta admit that the many hundreds of times I dreamed about your death, I never thought it would be like this."

Debs jackknifed into an upright position then locked eyes with Einstein, so fast it startled him and he fell onto his butt. How did this woman come back to life without electricity?

"Something smells… *delicious*," she said.

Einstein sniffed. He wouldn't call any of the various odors permeating his workshop *delicious*. Unless you had a thing for gunpowder, solder flux, and 40 weight oil.

"I don't smell nothing," he said. "And, not that I'm complaining, but weren't you dead just a second ago?"

Debs opened her mouth like she was going to scream—

—but instead of screaming, she lunged forward and bit him.

On Her Boat…

Before jumping back into the water to chase after her two grandsons, a bright yellow weasel zoomed across her feet until it magically stopped on her pinkie toe.

She'd owned that boat for ten years, and never had any sort of rodent problems with it before.

Upon further scrutiny, she realized the weasel wasn't a weasel after all. Turned out to be that same minnow-shaped lure which had been lodged in her dominant cooking hand. Now it was stuck in her favorite foot! She yanked out the pesky treble hook, not feeling anything other than a mild itch as it tore a small hunk of flesh from her foot, and at the same time heard Randall's yell echo across the lake.

That boy sure did yell a lot.

The lure in her hand twitched, and after a moment of surprise, she figured out the meaning behind it and was delighted.

I've taken my grandsons fishing countless times. But this will be the first I'm fishing for my grandsons.

She began to pull in the line, gathering it around her hands, grinning and (shamefully) drooling a little as she watched Randall and Josh get pulled closer.

My my my. This is a big one.

A keeper for sure.

She hadn't felt this pleased since retiring from her job as Fire Chief and receiving her first pension check.

Randall struggled to keep above the surface as Grandma dragged him closer and closer. But she wasn't alone in her quest to eat those delectable children. Other hungry swimmers were converging as well.

"Stay away from my little dumplings!" she called to the crowd. "Go eat your own grandkids!"

"They're big enough to share!" someone shouted back.

She saw it was her neighbor, Mildred Kanipple, who beat her last year at the Niboowin Apple Pie Bake-Off, taking both the town glory and a fifty dollar gift certificate to Merl's Sparkly Glue Stick Store. The woman was as flaky as her pie crust, and the rivalry was bitter.

"Mildred Kanipple, you keep your distance!" she warned.

"Or you'll do what? Get second place again?" Mildred cackled. "You should come over sometime and admire at my armoire. I covered the whole thing in silver glitter!"

"Go cover your head in silver glitter, you old goat! You'll need a case of it to fill in all those wrinkles!"

Grandma began to pull quicker, taking in two feet of line at a time. Though she always preached to Randall and Josh about the importance of sharing, the deep down hungry she felt washed away all considerations of generosity.

She had never been this hungry. Not even when she was on that fad Celery Diet back in the 70s.

When she finished hauling those grandkids into the boat, she wasn't going to share one single piece.

They are mine and mine alone. And I am going to savor every…

Single…

Bite!

In the Lake with Randall…

According to Josh's precise calculations, impeccable logic, and above-average brain chemistry, he and his older brother Randall were going to be zombie food.

Josh knew his body was made-up of sixty-five percent of water, but that didn't make swimming in it any easier. After getting attacked and pulled under earlier by Bob, that bearded old ghoul, Josh had vowed to never dip a toe in agua again. Yet here he was, in the lake and bobbing like—well—a bobber, while dozens of undead closed in around him and Randall and Grandma pulled them toward the boat.

"Cut the line!" Josh yelped.

"I left my Swiss Army knife at the house!"

Grandma gave a particularly vicious tug on the line, yanking Randall underwater. He broke the surface a moment later, spitting water and gasping.

Josh put his hands under his brother's armpits and kicked his little legs as hard as he could, aiming for the shore. Incredibly, he slowed their advance, and Grandma began to struggle with the fishing line.

But it was still a no-win scenario. The other zombies were still swimming toward them, and Josh was quickly running out of the little bit of reserve energy he still had.

"Thin line…" Randall sputtered. "It's biting… into my skin…"

Biting. That was an idea.

But if Josh was going to try to bite the line, it meant diving underwater.

Which meant taking off the lifejacket.

The thought terrified Josh. Being devoured by zombies was bad, but drowning was even scarier.

Then Randall got dragged underwater again, yanked right out of Josh's grasp.

And this time, Randall didn't come back up.

Josh fought panic. He screamed his brother's name at the wavy surface of the water, and before he knew what he was doing Josh's hands had unbuckled the lifejacket.

After taking the biggest breath he ever took in his life, Josh went under.

The lake was murky, and somehow seemed to have gotten colder. He squinted, but couldn't find Randall. He looked left, and right, and left again, and had no idea what to do until a column of air bubbles rose up a few feet directly ahead.

Josh swam toward the bubbles, kicking hard, and saw Randall, eyes wide, cheeks puffed out as he expelled precious O2.

He reached out for Randall's hand, caught it, then pulled himself down his brother's body, much like he would pull himself across the floating rope that sectioned off the shallow end from the deep end at the YMCA where he'd failed his swimming lessons. When he reached Randall's leg, Josh paused.

To bite the line, he had to open his mouth. If he did that, wouldn't all his air come out?

No. I can close my throat. My mouth will fill with water, but my lungs won't.

Right?

Josh wished he'd tested this hypothesis prior to that moment, to be sure, but already he could feel his heartbeat kicking up and his lungs whimpering for oxygen. He needed to do this. Fast.

Josh got his mouth near the musky line—

—opened his mouth—

—and didn't choke on the water.

His hypothesis had become a proven theory.

But he had no time to dwell on that small victory. He now had to try and bite through fifty pound test fishing line.

How hard could that be? Human beings had a hundred and twenty pounds of bite pressure. Should be easy.

Josh locked his choppers around the line and bit down.

It wasn't easy. Not even close.

Fifty pound line was based on tensile strength, not shearing stress. He might as well have been trying to bite through a steel cable. His molars weren't sharp enough.

As his brain began to be overwhelmed by air deprivation, Josh switched to using his incisors.

It still didn't work. And then the line was yanked out of his mouth. Josh caught sight of Randall's frantic face as he was pulled past him, and a panicking Randall seized Josh's arm, his fingernails digging into the younger boy's skin, and Josh let out a small yelp, along with some precious air, and that's when the obvious practically uppercutted his brain to space.

Fingernails!

Pulling himself alongside Randall once more, knowing they both would drown very soon, Josh once again reached the fishing line that ensnared his brother, held it with one hand, and began to pat down his swimsuit pockets with the other. There were strings in the elastic. Velcro. Nothing else. He checked again, this time really squeezing down on the fabric.

There!

Josh slid his hand down in his right pocket and wrapped it around the nail clippers. Dad didn't let him have a knife, but this was the next best thing. He pulled it out quickly—

—Randall was tugged away—

—and the nail clippers slipped from Josh's hand.

Nooooooo!

He watched the clippers begin to sink, quickly calculated the descent trajectory, and stuck his palm out underneath—

—making the catch.

This time he locked his legs around Randall so he wouldn't be ripped away, used both hands to open the clippers, and then placed them on the line where it looped around Randall's ankle.

SNIP!

And then they were free!

They both kicked for the surface, breaching like two skinny white whales, Josh blowing out carbon dioxide and sucking in delicious dioxygen, his all-time favorite allotrope.

As his lungs heaved, he turned to see lake water snot-rocket out of Randall's nose, followed by an extended coughing fit.

Josh looked around, searching for the life jacket, seeing it only a few feet away, reaching for it—and then shrieking in surprise.

The life jacket had a new owner. A bearded zombie named Bob that Josh knew all too well.

"You stole my nose!" the undead septuagenarian snarled, pointing at Josh. "Now I'm going to take yours!"

And the noseless monster began to doggie-paddle toward them.

On Her Boat...

Her stomach was rumbling like her old Dodge Rambler in need of a tune up, and she could practically taste her mouthwatering, flavorful grandkids, and then the line broke.

Grandma fell backward, landing in the boat seat. Rage boiled her insides. Her dinner had escaped. Didn't they know how hungry she was? How terribly bad she was starving? In all her years she'd never been this ravenous. Even when she was snowed-in during the blizzard of '67, and had been forced to boil and eat her tap shoes. Nothing could compare to the insatiable hole in her gut that needed to be filled.

Filled with young flesh.

Warm, chewy, flesh. Fibrous, stringy muscles. Crunchy bones. Soupy intestines. Gooey brains. Spongy kidneys. Even a sour gallbladder sounded good.

But instead of munching on energetic, youthful people-meat, she was watching her lousy neighbors encircle what—by blood relation—should have been her dinner.

She should have been the one to sink her teeth into those kids.

Teeth. Hmm...

She'd tried to bite Randall. Twice. And each time, her false teeth hadn't been up to the task. They might be good for slurping applesauce, or nibbling an occasional bismark, but they weren't suited for breaking skin.

Especially smooth, firm, Grandson skin.

She fondly remembered all of those fairy tales she'd read to the children when they were younger. They'd especially loved Little Red Riding Hood, when the wolf dressed up in Grandma's clothing to fool the kids and eat them.

The big bad wolf had no trouble at all gnawing through skin.

Why Grandma, what sharp teeth you have…

She plopped down on the chair behind the steering wheel and spat her slimy dentures into her palm. Inside her boat's compartment, beneath the dash, was a set of tools.

Grandma took the toolbox out, opened it up, and set upon finding the right one.

EINSTEIN

Wrasslin' with His Zombie Wife

Einstein found hisself in the unenviable position of pinned to the floor of his workshop, his undeadified wife straddling him. Debs was working her jaw like a snapping turtle training for the Olympics, and her strength was something spectacular.

Granted, Debs could beat him at arm wrestling four out of five times, but she tackled him like she had super powers, then bit his neck so hard it made him squeal like Ned Beatty.

There was a pulling sensation and a tearing sound, which abruptly stopped when she sat up, part of Einstein peeking out between her teeth.

"Gahhh! You bit off my neck mole!"

At least, Einstein assumed it was a neck mole. It first appeared a few months back, and had grown irregularly at an alarming rate, until it was roughly the size and shape of one of them GMO strawberries.

Einstein pushed her away, so fiercely he exemplified Newton's Third Law of Motion (for every action there is an opposite reaction) and he smacked his head on the floor of the barn. He blinked, hoping to see little cartoon birds flying overhead in a circle and tweeting, just like in the cartoons. There were no birds or tweets. Just blinding pain, and a warm sting in the moleless area on his neck.

He was disappointed at the lack of birdies. The cartoons lied yet again, just like that time he tested if getting hit in the face with a frying pan turned it the shape of a frying pan.*

Cupping his injury, Einstein struggled against dizziness and nausea and managed to sit up, focusing on Debs as she chewed on his mole like it was bubble gum. Blood oozed down the corner of her mouth, and her eye color had gone milky.

All at once, everything made sense.

"Cartoons aren't based on reality," he said. "That's why I've never seen a duck talk."

After that revelation, he had another.

"Did Clevis bite you, Debs?"

All signs pointed to Clevis's recently acquired cannibal affectation being contagious. If so, all Einstein had to do was fix his SA9 and shoot his wife to turn her back to normal.

But first things first…

Einstein held out his hand. "Honey, give me back my mole."

She stuck out her tongue, showing him the piece, which was already pretty chewed up.

"Debs, I can glue that back on. Give it to me and I'll find you something else to eat."

She shook her head. "It's really tasty."

"I ain't funnin' with you," he said, using his *I ain't funnin'* voice.

Then she swallowed it.

"Dang it, woman! That ain't right!"

Debs licked her lips. "It was mole-licious."

"Coulda been a tumor."

"It was tumor-iffic."

"Stop making up dumb words!"

Einstein scanned around for a weapon, and sighted his boomerang hammer. He reached for it, took aim, asked the good Lord to forgive him, and threw it hard as he could at his wife's face—

—and missed.

---

*It didn't.

A moment later, it hit him in the back of the head.

When Einstein opened his eyes, Debs was gnawing on one of his three thumbs. His favorite one. He pulled it out of her greedy mouth, gave her a kick, and then rolled over and crawled for his workbench.

She caught him by the leg, halting his progress, when he was only inches away from his self-made semi-automatic grease gun. It was the perfect defense against a zombie attack. One squeeze of that custom-designed hair trigger, and he'd be slipperier than a slime eel at a motor oil party. Einstein stretched, so hard his back crackled.

So close.... so close... just reach... a little bit... farther!

Just as Debs bit into his calf, he grabbed the grease gun, and it slipped out of his hands.

He grabbed for it again. It slipped again.

That was his problem. He was too darn good at genius inventions.

Einstein twisted onto his back, putting the heel to Debs's munchy face. Then he snatched up the grease gun, holding it really hard, and it slipped out of his hands and shot about eighteen feet across the floor.

Switching focus, he locked peepers on one of his favorite inventions; the automatic beer launcher.

He crawled for it, grabbed the end, and it slid away because Einstein's hands were still covered with grease. He wiped his palms on his bib overalls, grabbed it again, and then racked a warm can of beer into the chamber. Einstein pointed it at his wife.

"This Bud's for you."

He fired.

Nothing happened.

That's when Einstein remembered he could never get his automatic beer launcher to launch.

He considered giving up and drinking the beer, but decided it was too cowardly, and a bit too early in the evening to start drinking. Then he considered throwing the beer at her, but his head still smarted from the last thing he'd thrown. Then he considered sea otters. Those cute little rascals were the clowns of the ocean, and always brought a grin to his redneck face when he watched them on the Sea Otter Channel, free because he pirated cable TV through a complicated and dangerous splicing of wires. He also stole electricity, tying directly into the underground line that ran across the bottom of Lake Niboowin.

Einstein didn't steal natural gas, because he made enough of his own.

But getting back to his thought about sea otters. Sea otters wouldn't give up, probably. So Einstein decided to fight until he couldn't fight no more. That was how he'd acted throughout his married life, and that was how he wanted it to end. Debs might wind up eating him. Or a more likely scenario (since she'd bit him twice) was he'd turn into an undead ghoul like her. Which really wasn't fair. Marriage was supposed to be *till death do you part*. The idea he'd still be wed to Debs for another thousand or more years was downright disheartening.

So he couldn't give up. He had to fight Debs off, then use his genius intellect to cure them both so they wouldn't have to spend eternity annoying each other.

Einstein unloaded the beer, cocked it back to throw at his wife's head, and it slipped out of his hand. Because; grease.

"I tell you, Rupert. These last few years, you been about as useful as flippers on a polecat. But I think I finally found something you're good at." She grinned a bloody grin. "Dinner."

"You might eat my body, woman. But you'll never eat my pride."

"What pride? You're a dimwit and a screw-up."

"My legacy will outlive us both, even if we're zombies who live forever. This laboratory—"

Debs made her face. "It's a barn, you moron."

"—will someday be a shrine to my genius. People of the future will study my inventions. In fact, they might already have studied them, if they found my nacho-maker time machine."

That contraption, built out of aluminum siding and three and a half artificial Christmas trees, still had some kinks to work out. Firstly, he could only travel into the future the exact same number of minutes he sat inside the device. Secondly, it made cheese that tasted like feet.

Einstein doubted there was any point in human history, past or present, where feet-cheese was highly valued.

"Moron. They warned me not to marry you."

"Who did?" Einstein asked, curious.

"Everyone. My parents. Your parents. The minister. Strangers who came up to me on the street. They all said I was throwing my life away. But I told them all I knew what I was doing. Rupert was going places, I said. He had a good head on his shoulders, I said. And I was right."

Einstein was dubious. "You were?"

"Yep. That's gonna be the first thing I eat; your head and shoulders."

Einstein was confused, trying to understand the dandruff shampoo reference, and then all of a sudden Debs was swarming all over him, biting and clawing, and when she chomped on his neck again Einstein started to realize she wasn't referring to *Head & Shoulders* shampoo at all.

As the woman he'd sarcastically referred to for years as a *bloodsucker* began literally sucking his blood, Einstein tried to imagine what the wily sea otter would do.

That's it! I can use a rock as a tool to crack open an abalone shell!

Then Einstein passed out from blood loss.

RANDALL

Swimming with Josh...

Tired as I was (and I'd never been this tired before in my life), I could still swim faster than the horde of geriatric undead surrounding us. But Josh, without his life jacket, swam at the speed of someone drowning.

The new owner of Josh's life jacket—an elderly, bearded zombie named Bob who was missing a nose courtesy of Josh—was paddling his way, looking appropriately angry because of the nose thing.

"RANDALL!" Josh hollered, which wasn't necessary because I was only a few feet away from him. "HELP!" Calling for help was also unnecessary. For a smart kid, he needed to work on his grasp of the obvious.

I reached out and yanked Josh toward me just as Bob grasped for him. Then I put myself between the two of them and faced the senior citizen head-on.

"I want my nose!" Bob gurgled, spitting lake water.

Much as I wanted to give the man his nose back, it wasn't in my possession. Best guess, some hungry bass or snapping turtle gobbled that up a while ago. And Bob's crazed expression indicated he wasn't going to like that answer.

Think, Randall. Think.

But thinking wasn't my strong suit. Josh was right. My intelligence was about average, and that was on a good day. I had to get away from an angry, noseless dead man wearing a lifejacket, while also saving my near-hysterical brother, and the only average thought that popped into my average head was—

Hmm.

Could that actually work?

Only one way to find out...

I pushed my thumb between my index and middle finger. A classic trick to fool babies. Could it work on a voracious, zombie geezer?

"I got your nose!" I said, wiggling my thumb.

Bob reached a hand up to the ugly hole in the middle of his head, feeling around. Then his eyebrows crinkled.

"Give it back!"

"Go and get it!"

I held my fist high in the air and then pretended to throw it across the lake. While Bob watched, horrified, as his imaginary nose arced through the air, I grabbed a flailing Josh under the armpits in a lifeguard carry and began to kick hard.

After a moment of resistance, Josh got the idea, and began to kick along with me. I took a quick look behind me at our target—the pier we'd been casting for earlier. Twenty, maybe twenty-five yards away. Then I scanned the lake around me.

Grandma was still in her boat. She had the motor tilted up out of the water and was fiddling with the propeller. Trying to untangle Deonte's dreadlocks, no doubt. Around us, in a half-circle, were more swimming old folks. And where Bob was a moment ago... an empty life-jacket. He'd probably gone deep sea diving for his nose. I kept a lookout, waiting for him to come back up, but he stayed down. Could zombies drown? Even though it was mean to hope for it, I did anyway. That no-nosed dude seriously freaked me out.

The combined leg power of me and my brother made us faster, and we slowly pulled away from the pack. I glanced at the pier, only ten yards away. We were really cruising. And still no sign of Bob. He never could have held his breath for that long. He had to have either sunk, or given up.

For the first time since we'd run from Grandma's house, I allowed myself a small measure of hope.

I did it. We're actually going to make it. We're going to get out of—

With a violent jerk, Josh was ripped from my hands and sucked underwater. I caught his outstretched wrist and tried to pull, but whatever had him was stronger. I squinted through the murky water. Bubbles surrounded Josh's head as he screamed, wide-eyed. I swam my way down Josh's body, and almost cried out when I saw what had him.

Bob.

Gnawing on Josh's knee.

This day had easily topped my Worst Days Ever list. Fear, desperation, worry, despair, sorrow, guilt; I'd experienced so many negative emotions I felt like a squeezed sponge with nothing left inside.

But I did have something left.

Seeing Bob bite my brother made my entire body flush with red-hot rage.

I reached for him, my hands finding his nose hole, jamming a finger in. That got his attention. He ceased his attack on Josh, and reached for me, locking his fingers around my neck. I shoved Josh toward the surface with my free hand, and with my other I crooked my finger and yanked, trying to rip Bob's face off.

For a moment we were deadlocked, him squeezing, me pulling, and then his legs scissored around my waist and he locked his ankles.

Air squirted out of me like toothpaste from a tube. I immediately pushed against his knees, trying to get away as we slowly descended into the depths.

Oxygen-deprived panic took hold of me, and as I fought to keep air in my lungs, Bob smiled at me.

Why wasn't he fighting for air, too?

Then I remembered the comment Gustav made.

"I don't need to breathe, even though I do have to work the old diaphragm to be able to speak."

We continued to sink. My vision got dark.

There was no doubt about it. I was going to die.

In the Woods with Tom...

Barbara clutched her bandaged belly, putting pressure on the wound. It hurt, but she'd given birth to two children. A bite—no matter how vicious—didn't come close to the pain of six hours in labor.

They continued to head east, following the Google Map. The signal was gone, but Tom had taken a screenshot, and they determined direction by moving away from the setting sun.

Barbara had been leaning on Tom, an arm slung over his shoulder while he held her tight around the waist. Part of this was because her injury made walking painful. But it also felt good to be held. With each of them working full time, and two children, intimacy was a commodity. Their romantic picnic plans had ended in horror, but cleaving to her husband was a welcome consolation prize.

"I love you," she said.

He stopped, then smiled at her. "Love you, too. We'll get through this, babe."

"You sure?" Barbara wasn't so certain. Something felt... wrong. As if they weren't nearing the end of their ordeal, but rather it was only the beginning.

"We can do anything together. It doesn't matter if there are a hundred crazy old cannibals out in these woods—"

She shivered. "Don't even say that."

"I'm serious. We could be in the middle of a cannibal apocalypse, and we'd find a way to get through it. We're stronger than the sum of our parts."

He kissed her forehead, and for a brief moment Barbara felt that it might be true. That their combined strength would always win the day.

Four steps later, they saw the shoreline, and Barbara's hope became full-blown optimism.

Tom walked Barbara to a wide tree, which he leaned her against.

"Rest here, I'm going to see if I can flag down a boater."

"Don't leave me."

She reached for him, her wound stretching, pain stealing her breath.

"Careful! Don't rip the Band-Aid off. We don't want it to get infected." He grasped her elbow and helped her sit on the ground.

"What if the bite is infected?" she asked, staring up at him.

"It only just happened. And I have antibiotics at the cabin."

"Do you have a rabies shot?"

"You don't have rabies."

"Why else would someone try to eat me?"

"It was just a bite."

"It was several bites, Tom. Along with chewing, and swallowing."

Tom lost some color. "If it is rabies, they'll have medication at the hospital."

"What if it's something else? Something worse?"

"What are you saying, Barbara? The guy was just some nut. Maybe he escaped from a mental institute. Or the Niboowin Nursing Home."

"He wasn't just some old, crazy man. He shouldn't have been able to walk. His whole body was covered in burns. I don't even know how he could move."

"Third degree burns destroy nerves. Maybe he couldn't feel pain."

Barbara's tone sharpened. "Explain why his eyes were milky white."

"You were in shock. People in shock see things. Believe things that might not have happened."

Tom saying that was a punch in the gut.

"You think I'm lying?"

"Babe, of course not. I'm just saying you were delusional that's all. There's nothing wrong with that. That's human nature when stressful situations occur."

"Maybe human nature isn't the problem here."

"What are you saying?"

Barbara looked away. "Maybe he wasn't human at all."

Tom groaned. "What was he, Barbara? A vampire? A werewolf? I thought they only came out at night."

"That man was burned all over, Tom. He should have been dead. But he was walking."

"Walking dead? That's not real."

"I know what I saw."

"There has to be some other explanation, Barbara. Our life isn't some fiction story being told by a big shot author."*

"Dammit, Tom. Some old man who shouldn't have been even alive tried to eat me! I'm not insisting he was a zombie. But I'm not delirious and I'm not in shock and you need to believe me!"

A rush of blood flowed to her face, making her cheeks hot.

Her husband's face softened, and he reached for her hand. "I believe you, Barb."

"Tom…" She squeezed his fingers. "He's still out there. And our boys…"

Barbara's words trailed off as her mind tortured her with images of worst case scenarios.

"Josh and Randall are smart. They wouldn't mess with any strangers. And your mother is no wimp. Remember when we were first dating, and she bet she could lift me in a fireman's carry? Took me up a flight of stairs. She'll protect them. She's strong. And it runs in the family. You're strong. And our kids are strong. They'll be fine."

Barbara nodded, hoping he was right. But something in her—call it motherly instinct—told Barb that her children were in serious, serious trouble.

---

* And his son.

In the Lake with Randall…

They were in serious, serious trouble.

Josh couldn't see how bad his knee was, because of all the blood. But it hurt, and when he reflexively touched it, he felt a jagged flap of skin.

He was also cold. Very cold.

Could be shock, setting in.

But Josh's primary worry wasn't himself. It was Randall.

His brother was underwater, with Bob. Each second he didn't come up was torture.

C'mon, Randall. Come up.

Fight him and come up.

Please…

But Randall didn't come up. The only thing that breached the surface was bubbles.

Josh didn't know what to do. He was so cold. And so tired.

So tired that he didn't have the energy to thrash around and keep himself afloat.

And yet…

He wasn't sinking.

Deep down, Josh knew that his biggest hurdle in learning how to swim was overcoming his fear. The instructor at the YMCA had told Josh to *relax,* over and over, but Josh had always been fighting so hard to keep his head above water that relaxation was impossible. He prided himself on being rational, but fear overrode his intellect every time he was in water deeper than a bathtub.

But now he was too exhausted to struggle. And rather than drown, he was bobbing on the surface with minimal effort.

I can do it! I can swim!

And that meant…

I can save Randall!

Suddenly feeling strong, warm, and more grown-up than he'd ever felt before, Josh took a breath so big it hurt, submerged, and searched underwater for his big brother, finding Randall only a few feet beneath him.

Josh kicked harder, pointing his toes and keeping his legs straight, pulling himself through the water with cupped hands. When he reached Randall, Josh saw that Bob had locked his legs around his brother's waist. Randall was trying to push himself free, but it was a losing battle. Bob was bigger and stronger. Josh knew there had to be a smarter way.

From all prior indications, zombies didn't feel pain. But they must have retained some sort of central nervous system for their muscles to still work.

Rather than try to hurt or overpower Bob, Josh went right for his armpits, digging his fingers into Bob's radial nerves—

—and tickling him.

Bob's reaction was immediate. He released Randall and began to convulse in silent, underwater laughter. Randall kicked for the surface, and Josh was right on his heels, and then they broke the surface and saw the pier, ten meters away.

They swam for it. But it wasn't a lame, little kid doggie-paddle. And Randall didn't need to help. Josh matched his brother, stroke for stroke, in an overhand crawl, swimming like he'd been born in the water, and actually beating Randall to the dock.

As soon as he pulled himself up, everything began to spin. Adrenalin reserves depleted, Josh collapsed onto his back, staring at the setting sun. It would be dark soon. Dark, and rainy.

Randall hacked up lake water, snorted and spat. Then spun around to see the zombies.

"We got about a two-minute window," He slid off his shirt, wrung it, and gently wrapped it around Josh's throbbing knee.

"How bad is it?" he asked.

"Little scratch."

"Really? It's that bad?"

"You're overreacting, like you always do."

Though Randall was downplaying the injury, Josh saw the worry on his face.

"Did you stop the bleeding?"

Randall finished tying the overhand knot. "Yep."

"Did you see the patella?"

"The what?"

"The kneecap," Josh said.

"It's not that bad, Josh. You're going to be—"

"A zombie," Josh interrupted. "I'm going to be a zombie."

Randall shook his head. "Don't say that."

Josh knew better. "Grandma was bit. She became a zombie. Same thing is going to happen to me."

"Wrong. Have you seen how many times Grandma bit me?" Randall pointed at himself, "my ear. My neck. Basically my whole face. Out of all people to become a zombie, it should be me. Yet, here I am, on the road again."

For a second, Josh's heart soaked with hope, but his brain calculated different.

"Her dentures fell out," he said. "She didn't pierce your skin."

"How about her spit? That could've entered my nose or mouth somehow."

"Randall, that's not how—"

"You're not dying on me!" Randall's eyebrows creased. "You got that? We'll do whatever it takes."

His eyes looked determined, and Josh felt a sudden responsibility for not only himself, but for Randall. "We may have a chance, depending on how fast the infection spreads."

"What do you want me to do? Amputate your leg?"

"Gah! No! Get me to a hospital and give me antiviral drugs!"

"What about anti-SpongeBob-biotics?"

"Bovine *spongiform* encephalopathy is mad cow disease. It's a prion."

Prion disease couldn't be cured. It couldn't even be treated. But Josh saw no reason to worry his brother with that possibility.

"How do we get to a hospital?" Randall asked. "Nearest one is over half an hour's drive from here."

Josh looked around, his eyes settling on an all-too-familiar cabin.

"Help me up," Josh said. "I have an idea."

Still in the Woods with Tom…

"You see our house, yet?" her husband asked, holding her waist.

Barbara chewed on her thumb and mumbled, "I'm looking."

Lake Niboowin was a two hundred acre kidney-shaped body of water with a peninsula of forest indenting a third of it. Around the perimeter, log cabins with boat docks neighbored every fifty to a hundred feet.

Barbara tried to get her bearings, hunting for a two-story brown log cabin with a wide white pier docking a black bass boat. While on the lake, she could find her way back to Mom's with her eyes closed. But from an unfamiliar section of shore, it was confusing.

Tom squinted at his phone. Since reaching the lake, one bar of signal had been winking on and off. They'd tried calling the cabin, but the phone was busy.

"Don't all phones have call waiting?" he said, anger in his voice.

"It may be off the hook. Try 911 again."

"Hold on. Lost the signal."

Barb continued to scan the lake. She saw one boat, way in the distance, and a lot of small dots in the water.

Loons?

Swimmers?

It was odd.

"911 is a recording." Tom smashed the end button, and his lips went bitter.

"Try Randall."

"Lost the signal again."

Looking… looking… looking.

A-ha!

"Found it!" Barbara tapped Tom's shoulder while pointing at the cabin. "It's only about a hundred yards away."

Tom followed her finger. "We can follow the shoreline. Can you make it?"

Barbara nodded.

"There are three houses between ours and here. We could bang on doors, see if anyone is home, break in to use their phone if we need to."

"I can make it. I want to get to our family."

Tom put one arm around her waist, his free hand searching for a cell signal, and they began to walk. After a few steps, Tom stopped.

"Got a bar. Trying Randall."

"Put it on speaker."

Barbara listened to the phone ring four times, then got to her son's voicemail. That was odd. Randall took his cell everywhere.

Tom was obviously thinking the same thing, because his face was creased with worry. "Maybe he's charging it."

"Try Josh."

The phone rang once.

Twice.

Three times.

Then the ringing stopped.

"Did he pick up?" Barbara asked.

"Hello?" Tom said. "Josh? Can you hear me?"

Silence.

"Was the call dropped?"

Tom squinted at it. "Says it's connected. Call is live. Josh? Hello?"

A small, frail voice answered, "Is that you, Dad?"

What an odd thing to ask. Didn't he recognize his own father?

"It's me, son. Is Grandma okay? She didn't answer the house phone."

No answer.

Barbara glanced at Tom. "Is the volume up?"

"Didn't you just hear it ringing? We could hear it fine."

Barbara pursed her lips so she didn't snap at him. Tom caught the look and pressed the volume button. It was set on max.

"Josh, baby, answer me." She glanced at Tom. "Bad signal?"

Tom cleared his throat, "Josh! Son! You there? Everything okay?"

"I'm scared."

Barbara had never heard Josh sound so frail. "What's wrong? Where are Randall and Grandma?"

"I dunno. They're not here."

"What's wrong, Josh? Tell Mommy what's wrong."

"Please come home, come home. I'm alone. And something bad happened to Grandma."

Barbara could feel her chest constrict, and her bite wound seemed to throb harder. She stared at Tom for reassurance, but he looked as shaken as she felt.

Tom cleared his throat again. "Watch out for strangers, Josh. Don't let anybody inside. We'll be home in ten minutes."

"I think someone's at the door. Is that you?"

"That's not us, Josh!" Tom yelled. "Don't—"

The call disconnected.

"Call nine-one-one, Tom."

"I lost the damn signal again." His eyes searched hers. "I can move faster than you, but I can't leave you here alone."

"I'll be one step behind you."

He grabbed her hand and dragged her along the shore. Barbara pressed her hand against her injury, feeling warm blood soaking through the bandage. But she kept pace with her husband, pushing herself as hard as she could.

They ran until the shoreline depth dropped to calf-level, the water tangled with lily pads. Tom took her hand and pulled her up and onto a pier—Barb recognized it as the Patel's who lived two doors down. She ran up the stairs leading to the house, onto the patio, seeing the grill covered, the deck chairs stacked, the shades drawn; all signs that the neighbors had left for the season.

Tom at her heels, Barbara jogged around the cabin, reaching the access road. Mud Lane. It was sand and gravel, not asphalt, but much better than uneven forest or boot-sucking beach, and they were able to increase their speed.

Each step was an agonizing blend of fear, worry, and pain, and even though they were making good time, Barbara felt like she was wading through molasses while wearing lead shoes.

Not soon enough, Grandma's cabin came into view, their white SUV still parked in front. Tom extended his stride, sprinting ahead, leaving their backpack on the recently mown lawn as he rushed for the front door.

"Josh! I'm coming, son!"

Barbara scooped up the backpack as she jogged past, and came up next to her husband as he shook the door by the handle.

"Keys," she said, breathing hard as she offered the bag.

Tom unzipped it and pawed through the contents, finding the keys to the front door, taking far too long to open the lock, and then they were inside Grandma's cabin.

"Josh!" Tom yelled.

"Randall! Mom!"

"I'll take the upstairs," her husband said, already three steps toward the staircase.

Barbara locked the door behind her, then hurried into the living room, spotting the cordless phone on the floor. She picked it up and put it to her ear, pressing buttons.

Dead battery.

That's when she saw the blood on the floor.

There were smears in a repeating pattern, every few feet, and Barb realized they were footprints.

Someone was injured. One of the kids? Her mother?

Besides the blood and dead phone, a sofa cushion was on the floor.

Barb heard her husband calling for the boys, and then she ran into the kitchen.

It looked like a hurricane had swept through. Drawers and cabinets open, things strewn everywhere, and in the center of the room on the floor...

Barbara gasped in horror.

Blood. So much blood. And in the middle of the pool, a crimson-soaked throw pillow.

"Tom!" she called, but her throat was tight and it didn't come out any louder than a squeak.

She heard her husband run down the stairs. "You find anything? I'm checking the basement."

Then there was a scratching sound.

Barb looked around.

Scratch.

Scratch scratch.

It was the walk-in pantry.

"Josh?" she whispered, still too in shock to talk normally.

Scratch.

Scratch scratch scratch.

Barb swallowed, tried again. "Josh?" A bit louder this time.

Scratch.

Then a child's voice. "Mommy?"

Barb raced for the pantry, ready to pull open the knob—

—but she stopped herself.

Something was... wrong. Josh didn't sound like Josh.

He sounded like a cartoon character.

"Josh, are you in there?"

No answer.

Scratch scratch.

Maybe he's hurt. I'm being ridiculous.

Barb turned the knob, but again she stopped herself before opening the door.

"Josh, are you okay, baby?"

"I'm scared, Mommy."

All the tiny little hairs on Barbara's arms stood up. That definitely didn't sound like Josh.

So who's in the pantry?

"What day is your birthday, Josh?"

No answer.

Scratch scratch scratch.

"Josh? Do you know your birthday?"

"Happy… birthday… to me," he sang.

It was the creepiest thing Barbara had ever heard. Fear rooted her to the spot. She couldn't even draw a breath.

"Happy birthday to me. Happy birthday dear Josh. Happy… birthday… to… me."

Barbara lowered her eyes, staring at her hand, trying to make it let go of the doorknob.

"There's a broken light bulb down here!" she heard Tom call from the basement. But it seemed so far away. Miles and miles away…

"Know what I want to eat on my birthday, Mommy?"

"And blood!" Tom said. "The laundry room door is broken! You find anything up there?"

"Here's what I want to eat," said the thing pretending to be Josh. "I want to eat… YOU!"

The pantry door shot open, hitting Barb in the forehead, knocking her down, into the puddle of cool, coagulating blood.

Someone stepped out of the dark pantry. Someone much larger than an eight-year-old boy.

"Hi, Mommy."

Standing above her was a salivating old man with milky eyes and bloody clothes, wearing Josh's baseball cap.

"Something happened to Grandma," he said in his little-kid voice. Then he licked his teeth. "I bit her. I'm a baaaaaad boy, Mommy."

"Tom!" Barbara screamed. But it didn't sound like a scream. More like a cough.

"How was I?" the man asked, now using a deep baritone. Barbara saw he had a Niboowin Nursing Home nametag that read Gustav. "I haven't imitated children in a long while. I hope you don't mind me borrowing Josh's hat." He touched the brim, tipping it. "Method acting. Helps me get into the role."

"Where are my children?" she said, her voice stronger.

"Won't you read me a bedtime story?" he cooed, imitating Josh again. "How 'bout... the VERY HUNGRY CATERPILLAR!"

Gustav stretched his red mouth open as wide as a scream—

—and pounced on her.

In His Barn Workshop...

Einstein was having one of his self-defeatin' dreams, where he was trying to grab a fish in a tank that he needed for some strange dream-reason. But every time he caught the sucker it slipped out of his grasp and bit him in the hand.

"You're all thumbs!" the fish teased, spitting water in his face.

"Liar! I only got four thumbs!"

"You're not no genius, Rupert. You got less smarts than a bag of apples."

That insult hurt, because Einstein had a severe dislike of apples, going back to his youth. That's when Pa ran him over with an apple cart. Pa said it was an accident, but he did it four times. Even now, more than sixty years later, whenever Einstein saw an apple pie he had the urge to duck and cover.

The dream fish obviously knew this, mocking his shortcomings just like dream fish always did.

Einstein grabbed for the fish again, and again it bit his fingers and squirted more water.

"You're so stupid, you don't even know this is a dream!" the fish taunted.

"Do too! I can wake up anytime I want!"

"So go ahead and wake up!"

"Fine! I will!"

The fish spit in his face once more, and Einstein woke up, lying on the floor of his workshop.

Turned out it wasn't water squirting at him. It was blood. His own blood, coming from the stump in his hand where one of his thumbs used to be.

Einstein looked around and saw Debs sitting next to him, nibbling on his thumb like it was a buffalo wing.

"Dang it, Debbie-Sue Ellie-May Bobbie-Jo Franklin-Jane! Gimme my thumb back."

Debbie-Sue Ellie-May Bobbie-Jo Franklin-Jane did not give his thumb back. Instead, she swallowed it. And that was his favorite thumb, too.

Einstein sat up, feeling dizzy, and also feeling wet. He tried to recall, if sometime during his self-defeatin' dream, he went to the restroom, because sometimes, after too many beers, peein' in dreamland equated to *nocturnal enuresis*, which was a fancy scientific way of saying he needed rubber sheets after a night out drinkin' with Clevis.

Happily, Einstein's pants were only soaked with his blood. After blowing out a breath of relief, he managed to crawl over to a stray roll of duct tape, wrap a quick seal around his bleeding hand (which was tough to do with a bleeding hand), and also patch up the still-leaking bite on his neck.

Suitably repaired, he cast a wide glance around his back, looking for something to dissuade his zombie wife from eating any more of him.

Then it came to him, like a sign from above.

It was a sign, from above. Hanging on the ceiling, in bright red letters.

MAXIMUM LOAD FIVE HUNDRED POUNDS.

The sign was for his complicated block and tackle pulley system, which used an outboard motor as a winch. Einstein had hauled up Clevis with it, to give him a jolt of life-infusing lightning. If he could get those chains around Debs, he could hoist her up and keep her from snacking on him while he worked on perfecting his cure.

But how could he get close enough to tie her up? Zombified Debs was stronger than him. Even non-zombified Debs was stronger than him. He'd have to come up with some genius outsmarting scheme to trick her.

After considering several brilliant options, he went for the best one.

"Hey, Debs. Want to go for a block and tackle ride?"

Debs jumped on him and began biting his face, which Einstein took to be a *no*.

Luckily, he was so slick with his own blood, she couldn't get a good grip on him. Einstein slipped out from under her, somehow managed to twist around and get to his feet, and then he was half-stumbling/half-weaving toward his Corner of Shame.

He called it his Corner of Shame because that's where he tossed his genius inventions that didn't work right. Scanning over them quickly, he searched for something suitable to this particular situation.

Remote Controlled Bear Net?

Handcuff Slingshot?

Instant Mummy Wrapper?

Finding what he needed, Einstein picked up the contraption and whirled around, facing his undead wife.

"Hold it!" he warned, brandishing his Coffee Maker Pogo Stick. "How about a nice cup of joe?"

Never one to resist the allure of java, Debs halted her pursuit and held out her palm.

Einstein flipped the switch, and, incredibly, his contraption quickly brewed an aromatic mug of wakey juice. Just like it was supposed to. Then Einstein hopped onto the pogo stick part, and hot coffee splashed all over him.

As he screamed, slapping at the boiling liquid like it was flames and only succeeding in bruising himself where he was scalded, Debs lurched for him—

—then slipped on the coffee.

She went down, hard, banging her head on the ground something fierce and knocking herself out.

It had been a perfectly executed plan.

Einstein didn't hesitate to spring into action. Quick as a panther, he changed out of his coffee-stained shirt and his bib overalls, and then rummaged through a pile of old clothes for something comfortable yet stylish. But not too stylish; Einstein tried to cultivate a sporty yet laid back look. One that said, I look good, but I don't try too hard or spend a lot of money. He settled on an old exterminator jumpsuit that he got for free from the garbage because it was soaked with carcinogenic pesticides. After spending a few minutes dabbing oil on the zipper to get it to zip a little quieter, then another few minutes trying to get out the oil stains, he remembered that Debs was trying to eat him, so he put a strip of duct tape over her mouth so she couldn't bite him again (and also because it was something he'd wanted to do since they been married.)

Then he wrapped her in chains, started the outboard motor, and hoisted her up to the rafters mere seconds before she woke up and began thrashing around.

Just in the nick of time.

"There," he said, inordinately pleased with himself. "I'm finally safe."

That's when the horde of zombies came rushing through his open barn door.

In the Cabin...

The door to the basement laundry room was in pieces. It looked like a wild animal had clawed through. Horrible scenarios played out in Tom's head. The maniac who attacked Barbara getting into the house, chasing her mother and the kids. They hid in here, and then...

Not wanting to, but knowing he had to, Tom searched around for blood. Rage bubbled up inside him. The thought of anyone harming his children made him clench his fists.

He felt a cool breeze, looked up, and saw the basement window was open. Josh and Randall went in there sometimes, looking for frogs. Had they used it to escape?

"Josh!" he called, cupping his hands around his mouth.

No answer.

"Barb!" he called to his wife, upstairs, "I'm going outside!"

Tom climbed into the window well, and then out into the backyard. Dusk was coming on fast, pink and orange hues illuminating the westward horizon as the sun melted into the earth. The lake was a whole different world at night. Cooler, quieter, and somehow much larger and emptier. When Tom had been Josh's age, he'd had a primal fear of the dark.

Scratch that. He'd had a primal fear of what was *in* the dark.

Boogeymen. Monsters. Wild animals. Ghosts. Demons.

Zombies.

Unseen things, waiting to pounce.

"Randall! Josh!"

Tom jogged over to the back patio, then looked down at the lake. Grandma's bass boat wasn't tied to the pier.

He ran down the stairs, all the way to the end of the dock, and began to scan the water. Tom thought he could see a boat, several hundred meters away, but couldn't make out who was in it.

His mother-in-law had binoculars that she used for bird watching. Tom turned around, heading back to the cabin, and caught a strong whiff of BBQ.

BBQ gone slightly spoiled.

He got to the porch, reaching for the sliding glass door that led into the kitchen.

Pulled the handle.

Locked.

He rapped his knuckles against the glass, unable to see inside because the curtains had been drawn.

"Barb? You in there?"

Barb didn't answer. But Tom thought he heard movement inside.

"Barb! Boat is gone. Where does your mother keep the binoculars?"

There was a faint, high, squeaky sound. Sort of like a kitten mewling.

Grandma didn't have a cat.

Tom knocked harder. "Barbara?"

Another, louder noise. A cough.

What the hell?

Then, a series of thuds. Like someone pounding a nail with a hammer.

"Barbara, answer me!"

Something was wrong. He tugged hard as he could on the sliding glass door handle, pounded on it when it refused to budge, then vaulted the porch railing, beelining for the front door. His mother-in-law had towering stacks and stacks of firewood alongside the house; seriously, that woman swung a mean axe and had chopped enough to heat a small city for a year. Darting around the piles sent Tom into the thick pine trees on the property's edge, and two steps in the visibility dropped to zero.

Tom slowed down, waving his hands out in front of him so he didn't do a header into a tree trunk, then realizing how ineffective waving your hands out in front of you was when he took a header into a tree trunk.

The woods momentarily lit up as bright motes exploded in Tom's vision. He fell to the forest floor, landing on some lumpy pine cones, his head singing the pain song. In that moment, Tom lost all bearings and forgot where he was. Blinking didn't help; it was too dark to see.

The confusion, and the darkness, brought back fearful memories of his childhood. Of sleepless nights during thunderstorms, and being afraid to fall asleep in case the nightlight burned out and the thing under the bed could get him.

Jing-a-ding-a-ding.

What was that sound?

Tom sat up, and the quick motion brought dizziness, and nausea. He reached for his forehead, found a growing bump dead center.

Ding-a-ding-a.

He looked around, a useless effort in the dark woods. Then Tom switched senses, concentrating all of his focus on his ears, trying to locate the jingling sound.

Jing. Jing-a-ling.

A familiar sound. Like tiny bells. Tom couldn't discern the direction. But it was getting louder.

That meant it was getting closer.

Ding-a-ling-a-ling-a.

What was that? It sounds like…

Jing-a-ding.

Keys. Someone shaking a ring of keys.

And that rotten BBQ smell was getting so strong, Tom almost gagged.

The memory hit like a lightning bolt, making all of Tom's muscles go rigid.

Barbara stabbed that crazy old burned man with her keys.

Tom heard an exaggerated sniffing sound. Not like someone had a runny nose. But like someone was taking a long, pleasurable whiff of Thanksgiving turkey.

"Young man," said a monster in the darkness, "you smell like a big bowl of mac 'n cheese. And besides cough drops, them's my favorite thing to eat."

And then the monster fell on him.

Getting to Safety...

Still damp from the lake and the falling drizzle, my arm around Josh's waist, I half-carried him into the barn, skidding on my heels when we saw Miss Debra hanging from the ceiling, thrashing and spitting. She'd been turned into a zombie.

"You'll never take me alive, you thumb-eating demons!" Mr. Einstein yelled at us. Then he hopped onto some weird-looking pogo stick, splashed hot coffee all over himself, and began to scream.

"Mr. Einstein!" I yelled above his shrieks. "It's Randall and Josh, from across the lake."

Mr. Einstein stopped slapping his body and stared at us, cock-eyed.

"Randall and Josh?"

I nodded. "From across the lake."

"From across the lake?"

"Remember? You made us that fishing reel with the 96:1 gear ratio. One crank and it would reel in forty feet."

Mr. Einstein slapped his thigh and pointed. "Oh, yeah! How'd that reel do for you?"

The reel brought the lure in at about fifty miles-per-hour, much too fast for a fish to grab. Then it started on fire.

"Uh, great," I said. "We didn't mean to run in here without knocking, but we need help."

"It was my idea," Josh said. "If we have to fend off a zombie apocalypse, your place is the best on Lake Niboowin."

"Zombie acapo—wait one sec! Have you boys been zombified?"

"No, we—"

Before I could finish, he jumped on his pogo stick again, hollering and whimpering as he covered himself in more scalding coffee. Josh and I knew Mr. Einstein was an eccentric who fancied himself an inventor, but I couldn't figure out what the heck that pogo thing was. A training device that punished people who liked to bounce?

"Are you addicted to coffee, Mr. Einstein?" Josh asked.

"Owww! Huh? Whaddya say?"

"That invention you're riding. I'm guessing you're trying to wean yourself off of caffeine, so you built that for Pavlovian negative reinforcement. Every time you get on, it burns you, so your brain associates coffee with pain."

"Yep, that's what it is," Mr. Einstein said, letting the pogo stick fall to the ground. "And it works. Ain't never gonna drink coffee again."

"Your neck is red," I said.

"And I'm damn proud of my redneck heritage, so mind your mouth, young mister."

"I meant it's bleeding."

He touched the duct tape around his throat. "Oh. That. Wife got all bitey. Had to use the winch on her."

He jerked a thumb over his shoulder at Miss Debra, swinging from the rafters.

"You've got a combustion engine indoors?" Josh was looking at the outboard motor attached to the winch.

"Sure do," Einstein bragged.

"How about the dangerous carbon monoxide gas?"

"What now?"

"It can cause brain damage if you breathe it in too long."

"What now?"

"My brother is hurt," I interrupted. "Do you have a first aid kit?"

"What now?"

"A first aid kit," I repeated.

He struck a pose. "Son, I've got the best first aid kit in Northern Wisconsin. Follow me."

We tailed after him as he walked deeper into his barn, around boxes of junk. I took my time avoiding the spilled blood and sharp tools covering the floor.

"Watch out for this swinging live wire. Knocked into it once and I was bald for a year."

Josh especially avoided it, and even from five feet away I felt its steady thrum.

"And watch out for that poisonous poison venom in the box over there marked Tasty Treats. I should probably re-label that box."

I didn't know what I was expecting as far as first aid kits went. Maybe a heap of oily rags and a barrel of bleach. Or a sewing machine and a tub of baking soda. Or a box of antique bone saws and a tank of leeches. (There actually was a tank of leeches.) But I was shocked when he led us to a gigantic white bag with a telltale red cross on it. And it smelled brand new, not like the sourness of the rest of the barn.

"Ta-da!" he said with a hand gesture flourish. "The best first aid kit money can buy."

"It looks unused," Josh said.

"It is unused."

"But… don't you hurt yourself all the time?" Josh asked. "I mean, you're hurt right now."

"I know that," Mr. Einstein said. "I put the duct tape on myself."

"So why didn't you use your first aid kit instead of duct tape?"

"What? And get blood all over my first aid kit?"

When Grandma introduced us to Mr. Einstein, years ago, she said he was a really nice guy, but in order to relate to him you had to treat him like he was six years old.

"Good thinking," I said, tapping my temple.

Then Josh and I dug into the bag, laying out the supplies.

"Also, can you lock this place up?" Josh asked as we rummaged and sorted.

"Justa sec." Mr. Einstein limped over to the barn door and shut it, then shoved a bolt home. "Why, are more of those things out there?"

"About a hundred," I said.

"What now?"

"A hundred," I repeated. "Some of them have nametags from the nursing home."

He frowned. "Debs just came from the nursing home."

"We think it's some sort of pathogen," Josh said. "A disease."

"Some kind of zombie-itis?" Mr. Einstein asked.

"Something like that. Don't know if it's bacterial, viral, fungal, or a prion. Do you have any antibiotics?"

Mr. Einstein crossed his arms over his chest. "I don't believe in no drugs. Back in my day we had aspirin, and bicarb of soda, and people got along just fine. All of these designer prescription medications today, people paying seven hundred dollars a pill, it's just making Wall Street fat cats and insurance companies even richer while them pathogens you're talking about become harder to kill."

Somewhere in that rant there was probably some wisdom.

"When did you get bitten?" Josh asked.

"Dunno. Passed out for a bit. What time is it?" He checked the clock on the wall. "Almost seven-thirty. I'd say maybe half an hour ago."

Josh and I exchanged a nervous glance.

"How are you feeling?" I asked Mr. Einstein.

"Honest? I'm a little bloaty. Check the bag for bicarb of soda."

I poured hydrogen peroxide on Josh's bite. It's what we used at home for cleaning wounds, because it didn't sting like isopropyl alcohol.

"Are you… hungry?" I asked Mr. Einstein.

"Not more than usual."

I looked at Josh.

"I'm not hungry either," he said, making a *don't be an idiot* face.

"I'm not saying…"

"I know what you're saying, Randall. But I've been thinking. How many people live on Lake Niboowin?"

"Few hundred," Mr. Einstein said. "They aren't here all year round, but it's the end of the tourist season, so I expect a few dozen are still left."

"Kids?" Josh asked. "Teens?"

"All ages."

"But the only zombies we've seen are old."

"How old?" Einstein asked.

"Elderly."

"Define elderly."

"Past retirement," I said.

Einstein ran a hand over his stubbly face. I put some antibiotic gel on Josh's knee (Mr. Einstein's antibiotic prejudice was apparently limited to pills only), and then unwrapped a package of gauze.

"So," Mr. Einstein said, "would you say all of the infected have been over the age of sixty-five?"

I nodded. "Seems right."

"And you ain't seen no zombies younger than that?"

"No."

"And you, the little one, Ethan..."

"Josh."

"Andrew."

"It's Josh," Josh said again.

"Whatever. You got bit half an hour ago, and you ain't turned?"

"Are you saying the disease only effects geriatrics?" Josh asked.

"If'n you mean geezers, yep."

I finished wrapping Josh's knee up, then finally attended to the slash in my foot, when I stepped on the light bulb.

"How old are you?" Josh said to Mr. Einstein.

"I'll be sixty-five tomorrow," he said, smiling. Then he frowned. "Or is it today? What day is it?"

"Tuesday."

"I get the days that end in a *Y* confused."

"Every day ends in a Y," I told him.

"Quiet for a sec while I'm thinkin', Zeke."

"It's Randall."

"Shush now, Maybelline. I'm thinkin'. Now, Clevis turned sixty-five last month. Debs is sixty-six. They're both zombified. But I'm still sixty-four, and I got no desire to eat nobody."

I shook my head. "I really don't think this disease knows when people turn sixty-five. That's ridiculous. I'm no math or science wizard—

"I second that," Josh interrupted.

"—but how could some virus know your birthday?"

"Good point," Mr. Einstein said. "I don't know my birthday, neither."

"And what about leap years? Or daylight savings time? It makes no sense."

"Do zombies make sense?" Josh asked. "We're already suspending our disbelief in a big way. Why not take it a little further?"

"What are you saying?"

"I'm saying, Mr. Einstein may be onto something."

"It's my burden," Mr. Einstein said. "Cursed to be the smartest bulb in the knife drawer."

My brother and I ignored him. Above us, thunder cracked and the barn rumbled.

"Do you know what telomeres are?" Josh asked.

"Sure," I said. "We learned about them in class."

I hoped he didn't ask which class, because I had no idea what he was talking about.

"That's how you talk to each other long distance," Mr. Einstein said.

"That's a telephone."

"Right. It's the Spanish station on cable TV."

"That's Telemundo."

"Yeah. It's that noisy thing that Scottish men in skirts blow into."

"That's the bagpipes. Telomeres are the repeating nucleotide sequences on both ends of a chromosome."

"'Course they are," Mr. Einstein said. "I was just testing you."

"Each time a cell replicates, the DNA strands get a little shorter," Josh was using his lecture voice, the one he practiced for the future day he was invited to do a TED Talk. "Telomeres are like buffers. When the telomeres get shed during mitosis, there isn't any problem as long as there are more left. But when the telomeres run out, the cell doesn't replicate perfectly. Scientists speculate they're actually responsible for aging. Like a ticking biological clock."

"Right, the Spanish telephone clock," Mr. Einstein said.

"So you're saying these telomeres know when a person turns sixty-five?" I asked Josh.

"Why not? The idea is no crazier than anything else we've seen today. And it explains why Mr. Einstein and I haven't become zombies. We're not old enough. If the pathogen only effects cells that have shed all of their telomeres, we can't be infected."

"Until we're sixty-five," Mr. Einstein said.

"Exactly."

Mr. Einstein's face sank. "Uh, guys. I think I just remembered. Today is my sixty-fifth birthday."

I met Josh's nervous stare.

"Do you know what time of the day you were born?" Josh asked, measuring his words.

"I don't actually remember. I was very young at the time. But Pa was angry at me for years because when I was born I made him miss *The Lone Ranger* on TV. He used to hit me with a lead soup ladle and yell, *'Rupert, why weren't you born an hour later, at nine pm, so I didn't miss The Lone Ranger!'* He did it every day, until I turned eighteen and became a man." Einstein frowned. "Then he switched to a belt."

"So you were born at eight pm," Josh said.

"Math ain't my strong suit, but that seems right."

We all looked at the clock on the barn wall. It was sixteen minutes to eight pm.

"Well," Mr. Einstein said, "this really sucks the farts out of dead hogs."

On Her Boat...

It took a bit of doing, but she finally untangled all of the—was that hair?—wrapped around her propeller.

Once the motor was lowered back into the water, she gave the lake a long look to see where her grandkids were. Last she checked they were in the water, struggling to make it to shore. Josh had always been a poor swimmer. She half-expected him to be bobbing in the waves, facedown, his older brother sobbing next to him. Or maybe the other paddling old folks—every last one of them avaricious and selfish—had already begun to feast.

But there were no corpses, being snacked on or otherwise.

Though darkness was coming on fast, Grandma's eyesight seemed keener than ever. But her kin were absent everywhere she scanned.

Grandma considered cursing, but she'd weaned herself off that when she'd been Fire Chief, putting a swear jar in the station house and charging a dollar every time one of her team said a naughty word. They'd raised over six hundred bucks for charity, and she hadn't cursed since.

So instead she yelled, "Forking mother trucker fudge berries!"

It didn't have the same impact.

Taking a deep breath, she smacked her lips and realized that there was something in the twilight air.

Something… *tasty.*

Grandma took a big sniff, and found her sense of smell had improved as much, if not more, than her night vision.

I can smell the grandchildren.

But she couldn't figure out what direction the delectable scent was coming from.

"Attention!" she called out to her Lake Niboowin neighbors swimming all around her. "All of you greedy, hungry moochers! If you want to eat my grandchildren, help me find them! Sniff them out!"

The geriatric fleet around her began to snort at the air. Then a single, female voice rang out across the lake.

"I smell them!"

It was that danged Mildred Kanipple. Apparently the woman had a nose for adolescents just as sophisticated as her nose for apple pie.

Grandma scowled. "Which way?"

Mildred pointed—

—toward a stretch of lakeshore property. It belonged to that crackpot, Rupert, who called himself Einstein in what had to be the biggest misnomer in the history of nicknames.

Grandma sat in the driver's seat, started up her bass boat, and headed toward the moron's house. She figured she had at least a ten minute head start on the horde.

And hungry as she was, Grandma could devour both of her grandkids in half that time.

In the Kitchen…

Self-defense classes never taught Barbara what to do if a zombie tried to eat you after impersonating your boy.

But, they did teach her a few tricks.

As Gustav pounced, Barbara bent her knee and kicked, aiming for *his* boys.

She was stunned when he didn't buckle over, drop to his knees, and heave with agony. Instead, he barely flinched when he took the hit, and then his mouth twisted into a creepy grin.

"The lady doth protest too much, methinks."

Hell, Barbara hadn't even begun to protest…

She dropped to a crouch, stuck out her leg, and swept her boot behind Gustav's heels. He staggered backward, into the pantry, crashing into the fully-stocked shelves. The impact shook the stored foodstuffs, and a barrage of them dropped on his head, one by one.

A can of soup.

Another can of soup.

A jar of alfredo sauce.

A box of shell noodles.

The five pound can of tomatoes—

—didn't fall.

Gustav flashed his teeth and pushed up and off the shelves, regaining his footing. That prompted a bag of flour to upend and dump all over his head. His wet, milky eyes stared out through the white powder, making him look even more terrifying.

"By the… pricking… of my thumbs," he cooed. "Something… wicked… this way comes."

Backing away, Barbara cast her eyes around for some sort of weapon. She butt-bumped the center island. Turning, she picked up a toaster, and bounced it off the creature's chest to no effect.

He doesn't feel pain.

But there are other ways to stop an attacker.

Knock him down; go for the legs.

Blind him; go for the eyes.

There were a few more items on the island.

A cheese grater.

Maybe some other zombie fight.

A bunch of grapes.

Probably not an effective weapon.

Cooking oil.

What was she supposed to do? Fry him?

Salt and pepper shakers.

That'll work.

She quickly unscrewed the bottoms, then clutched the salt in her left hand, the pepper in her right.

"Excellent idea," Gustav said, running a slimy tongue over his lips. "I like a little seasoning on my food."

Barbara flung both of her hands outward, like she was cracking two whips. Trails of powder—one white and one gray—arced through the air and exploded in his face.

As Gustav pawed at his eyes, Barbara turned and ran for the patio door. Reaching for the handle, a pulsing stitch in her belly stole her breath.

She dropped to her knees, staring down her body, lifting her shirt and seeing the blood soaking through the bandage.

Barbara reached for the patio lock, but it wasn't there. Instead, there was a hole where the switch should have been.

"I'm sorry, Mommy," the creature said in its creepy little kid voice. "I broke the door. Please don't be mad."

Barbara reached for one of the island barstools, swung it hard at the patio door glass. It bounced off, and the reverberation caused her to scream in agony. She doubled over, clutching her wound.

"I can't see you, Mommy." Gustav began to move toward her, his hands still rubbing his eyes. "But I can smell you. You're bleeding bad, Mommy."

The only other way out of the kitchen was through the walkway, and Gustav had positioned himself between her and the living room. Though he still had his hands over his eyes, he was sniffing the air, and slowly moving in her direction.

"I can lick up the blood for you, Mommy. I won't hurt you… much."

Barb crawled around to the other side of the island, and he took two staggering steps toward her.

"Your blood… smells so good… so… so rich and spicy."

Biting her lower lip so she didn't whimper, Barbara lifted up her shirt and then unwrapped her soaked bandage. She balled it up and threw it over to the other side of the room.

Gustav changed directions, like a hound on a scent trail, homing in on the bloody fabric. He picked it up and held it under his nose, snorting.

"Clever girl," he said in his normal voice. Then he shoved the bandage in his mouth and began to chew, making *mmmm-mmmm* sounds as Barbara's blood oozed down his chin.

Barb tried to stand, but doubled-over immediately.

She considered her options.

Try to crawl away.

He'd catch her. If she didn't bleed to death first.

Hide.

He'd sniff her out.

Scream for Tom.

That would give away her location faster than the scent of her blood.

Fight.

Barb didn't have much fight left in her. She wasn't sure how much blood she'd lost, but it was enough to make her woozy.

Trick him.

Summoning up enough courage to speak clearly, she said, "Your imitation of my son… it's very good."

Gustav spit out her bandage. "Do you really think so?" he said, normally. "I haven't done any acting in years. I'm pleased I'm not rusty." He switched back to Josh. "Don't be afraid, Mommy. Dying doesn't hurt… much."

Barbara reached up and grabbed the cooking oil.

"That's… terrifying," she said.

"Why, thank you. I played a swamp creature in a 1960s horror film. I had to ham it up a bit, but the audience seemed to enjoy my portrayal."

"I believe it. I'm scared to death right now."

"It must run in the family. I scared your oldest boy so badly, I wouldn't be surprised if he wet himself. I didn't have to utter a single word, either. All I did was squeak a toy duck."

Barbara almost lost her shit right there. With tremendous self-control she asked, "You… attacked Randall?"

"Sadly, your children escaped in the boat. A shame. They smelled delightful. You have a similar scent. Like hot cross buns, fresh from the oven."

"And… my mother? Did you…"

Barb couldn't bring herself to say *eat her*.

"Your mother. Such a dear lady. She went after your children."

"She's with them?"

"I'm not sure. She made quite the effort, I can tell you. I heard her yelling from the middle of the lake. She was quite insistent that no one eat her grandkids…"

Good old Mom.

"…before she ate them herself," Gustav finished.

Barbara felt her throat get knotty. "My mother?"

"She's like me. Like the other hundred old souls at the Niboowin Nursing Home. We've changed. Been transformed. We're stronger. Healthier. More focused. And all so terribly, terribly *hungry*."

The thought of Mom turning into one of these monsters was worse than her being dead.

"How did she… become… a… a…" She couldn't even say it.

"I bit her."

Barb was torn between the agony over her mother, and the fact that she'd also been bitten. She let out a strangled cry.

"Don't you worry, young missy. You won't become one of us. You're not… how can I put this? *Mature* enough. We older folks, we're forced to look out for one another. No one else does, you see. Not our government, for sure, even though we paid our taxes and shoveled every spare dime into social security and Medicare. And not those we used to work for, who profited off the best years of our lives and put us out to pasture with embarrassingly inadequate pensions. And not the banks, who gambled with our money for decades while nickel and diming us with fees, forced us to pay exorbitant interest rates on houses and cars, and then offered us laughable returns on our life's savings IRAs. We never got golden parachutes. We were considered obsolete, embarrassing, and society marginalized us by treating those over sixty-five like children, abandoning us there so we wouldn't be a depressing reminder of *your* future."

Gustav stood up taller, sticking his chest out. When he spoke again, he was practically yelling. "They called us the Baby Boomers. We were once relevant. But then we fell victim to the universal bigotry. Ageism. The world thinks it has dismissed us. But we're still plentiful. And we're still strong. And we're going to show you youngsters just how strong we are. By eating every… last… one."

Chilled by his rant of geriatric Armageddon, Barbara had forgotten her escape plan. Then she remembered the bottle of cooking oil she was clutching in a death-grip.

"Were you ever in a musical?" she asked, trying to keep the fear out of her voice.

"What? Oh, yes. Many, in fact."

"Singing and dancing?"

"I was a countertenor, and could lindy hop with the best of them."

"What's a lindy hop?" Barbara quietly unscrewed the cap off the oil.

"Are you serious?"

"Can you show me?"

"You've temporarily blinded me."

"So you forgot how?"

"Of course not. That was a dance craze in my youth."

Gustav began to hum a swinging oldie, and then bounce around with considerable verve. The guy had some moves.

"That's good." Barb squirted the oil on the floor in front of him. "Do you know the twist?"

"Who doesn't know the twist? That's the biggest dance craze of them all."

Gustav began to twist like mad, contorting his ancient body like he was a teenager. Then the oil slick reached him. When Gustav stepped a toe into it he went ass over teakettle, cracking his head against the counter and falling onto his back, and becoming still. He was either unconscious, or dead.

In every horror film Barbara had ever seen, the victim fled as soon as the monster went down. But the monster always got back up and continued the pursuit.

That wasn't going to happen this time.

What Barb should have done was grab a cast iron frying pan, and flattened Gustav's head to the width of a pancake. But if Mom really had become one of these... things, then maybe there was a cure. So instead of bashing his brains out and possibly murdering an ill man, she went the more humane route and found a hammer and awl in the junk drawer.

She crawled to him slowly, quietly. Watching for any signs of movement. Carefully stretching out his leg, Barbara placed the point of the awl on his heel.

Then she hesitated. Fighting for your life was innate, and she'd honed those skills with self-defense classes. But committing violence against someone who wasn't fighting back gave her a sickening feeling.

Then she thought of her family, and found the strength to do the unconscionable.

Barb took a deep breath, and then nailed Gustav's foot to the kitchen floor as she screamed for Tom.

Tom did not come. But the nailing or the screaming woke Gustav up, he groaned, jackknifed into a sitting position, and reached for her, his hands grasping Barbara's hair.

"Don't you want to dance with me?" he grinned.

"Stop!" she yelled, quoting a dance craze from her own youth. "Hammer time!"

The face of her tool bounced off of Gustav's face, and bits of false teeth sprayed everywhere. It was like a volcanic denture eruption.

Gustav released her and cried out, "My teev! And my voot iv duck vo va voor!"

Hand pressed to her side, Barb crawled toward the living room, away from Gustav's whining. Rather than be overjoyed by her escape, she was more worried than ever.

Tom hadn't answered her screams. Which could only mean one thing.

Her husband was in trouble.

Barbara grabbed onto the counter and managed to get to her feet. She tore off half a dozen paper towels from the roll and pressed them against her bleeding wound. Clutching the hammer, she began to search for Tom. Then they'd find their kids, and somehow capture Mom.

Barbara had never been more certain about anything in her entire life. She was going to save her family.

Or die trying.

Next to Grandma's Cabin...

Pinned to the ground by a foul-smelling monster, Tom let out an uncontrollable, hysterical laugh, his eyes pooling with tears. Tom's inner child was overwhelmed by long suppressed fears. Fears that weren't supposed to really exist... but were now trying to *eat* him.

A set of uneven teeth cracked down on Tom's skull. Sharp pain fueled his panic, and Tom's thoughts spun until full-blown insanity was imminent. Then the ashy hands cupped under Tom's jaw and pushed up, exposing his neck, and clammy wet lips pressed against his Adam's apple.

That's when the biting began. Accompanied by a sound like someone slurping up an extra-long noodle.

Crazed adrenaline gave Tom a burst of super-strength, and he shoved the creature off him, pushing it off into the darkness.

Tom touched his neck, feeling blood and saliva.

Tinga-ling.

The jingling keys sound was to his left. Tom crab-walked right, bumping into a really wide tree. Stretching out his wingspan, he realized the tree was no tree at all.

Grandma's log pile.

Tom tried to control his hyperventilating in order to listen.

He didn't hear the keys.

Had they fallen out of the zombie's back? Or was it just standing very still, waiting to pounce again?

That's what the boogeyman would do.

Sliding along the pile, Tom let his outstretched right hand guide him. If he followed it to the end, he'd be by the front of the cabin. His left hand pawed the air, feeling for the zombie, not knowing what he'd do if he touched it. That thing was so strong. Not too heavy—Tom had been able to shove him off. But it had a grip like wood clamps. And a bite…

A bite like those imaginary monsters Tom had been afraid of as a child.

One step. Then another. Each bringing him closer to the front door. If he could get inside, lock the creature out, find some kind of weapon…

A weapon! Tom reached behind him, hefting a nice chunk of firewood.

He stopped.

Sniffed the air.

Overcooked bacon curled his nostril hairs.

"You can smell me," the darkness said. "I can smell you, too."

Tom couldn't tell where the voice was coming from. He listened for the jingling sound, but all he could hear was his own heartbeat, thumping like a bass drum.

"Your blood is tasty… like cherry cola."

Where was it? The darkness was messing with Tom's other senses. He continued to feel his way along the cords of wood, fingertips walking inch-by-inch.

Tom felt a set of eyes on him.

Boogeyman eyes.

Then he'd reached the end of the woodpile, and his fingers felt a different terrain.

Very different.

It wasn't the siding of the house like he hoped. Not a gutter. Not a corner.

It was mushy and wet.

And it had teeth.

Tom yelped, and pulled his hand away just as the cannibal snapped its jaws. Then he brought down the wood, the log slipping from his grip as he swung on open air. Tom reached behind him, grabbing another piece, and throwing it. Then another and another, the firewood crashing through the trees and brush, making no sound that he'd hit his target.

Damn the darkness. Tom would have killed for a flashlight, but it was in the backpack that he'd dropped and Barb had picked up. The bag also had waterproof matches in it; a colossal irony considering Tom was surrounded by firewood.

Why didn't cellphones have a match app?

Wait! He was such a moron! He had a flashlight app!

Tom slapped at his pockets, finding his cell phone, powering it on. The flashlight blazed to life—

—illuminating a grinning, barbequed visage straight out of hell.

"Fancy phone," the creature said, slapping it out of Tom's hands and plunging the woods into darkness once again.

Then it attacked.

Tom was yanked to the ground, pine cones crunching against his side. Tom kicked out, then the zombie pinned down his legs.

Teeth found his knee.

Then he heard a scream, coming from the house.

Barbara.

Tom thought he was using all of his energy fighting for his life, but when he heard his wife calling for him he found an inner strength he never knew he had. Pushing hard, Tom freed himself from the monster's jaws, twisted around, and felt for the wood pile. Rather than try to go around it, Tom began to climb.

Grandma could stack firewood as good as she could chop it, and the cord took Tom's weight without much shifting. When he got to the top, he braced his back against the side of the house and got his heels between the wood and the wall.

"You want to eat something, you bastard? Eat this!"

Tom pushed, so hard his ears popped, and two hundred cubic feet of wood rained down on the zombie.

As the logs fell, so did Tom. He rolled down the avalanche of timber, somehow landed on all fours, and then crawled toward the front yard.

"I'm coming, Barbara. I'm coming."

It seemed to take two eternities to reach the front door. And when Tom finally did…

Locked.

The thunder rumbled, shaking the sky. And then Tom heard the scariest sound ever.

Jing-a-ling-a-linga.

In Mr. Einstein's Barn…

Josh wasn't sure that his telomere birthday hypothesis was correct, but the only way to test it was to keep an eye on Mr. Einstein as the seconds ticked away to his sixty-fifth birthday hour.

"Uh, maybe we should restrain you," Randall said to Mr. Einstein. "You know, just in case."

"I dunno. I don't like being confined. That's why I sleep nekkid. Clothing restricts my preferred ability to spread out. I need my giblets to hang free."

Randall made a face. "We'll make sure your, uh, giblets aren't restrained."

Mr. Einstein nodded. "I 'spose it's probably best. Use that chain. And to be extra safe, there's a pick-proof padlock I invented, there on that barrel."

Josh lifted the lock, so large it filled his hand. It seemed sturdy enough.

"Where's the key?" he asked.

"Keys can be stolen or copied, so I never invented no key. That lock is 100% guaranteed theft-resistant."

"So how does it open?"

Mr. Einstein frowned. "Nevermind. Just wrap up my hands and legs with that roll of duct tape."

At five minutes before the clock struck eight pm, they had Mr. Einstein hogtied. If hogs were ever tied with duct tape.

"Now I want you kids to be brave. If I turn into one of them bitey creatures, I want you to take my SA—I mean my TCD9—and zap the bloodthirst outta me."

"TCD9?" Josh asked.

"The Cannibal Destroyer 9000," Einstein said proudly. "Over there, on my bench."

Randall and Josh went to the workbench.

"Looks like a shotgun," Randall said.

"Used to be, before my precise scientific modifications. But it shoots like a gun. Ever use a gun before?"

Both boys shook their heads.

"There are five rules you need to know," Mr. Einstein said. "First, the gun is always loaded. Never assume it ain't, and always check for yourself, then double-check. Second, never point it at nothing you don't want to kill. Third, don't touch that trigger until you're ready to fire. Fourth, know what's behind whatever you're shooting at, because you're gonna hit that when you miss."

"What's the fifth?" Randall asked.

"I refuse to answer on the grounds it will incriminate me," Mr. Einstein said.

Josh couldn't tell if that was a really clever joke, or not. Probably not.

"Go ahead, Warren, pick it up."

Warren—er, Randall—picked up the shotgun.

"Now push that lever on top. That'll open the breech."

The shotgun looked like it broke in half, but it was connected by a hinge.

"That was once my favorite double barrel twelve gauge. Those holes are where the shells went, before I did my genius conversion. What do you see?"

"Wires," Randall said. "And springs."

“The alligator clip on the end of the stock, you attach a cable to it, and it hooks onto a motorcycle battery. On the other end—”

“Wires are sticking out,” Josh said. He followed them across the floor of the barn and found some spiky, springy things that looked like you’d get tetanus if you touched them.

“Pick those up, Hubbard, and bring them here.”

“I don’t want to touch them,” Josh said.

“It’s okay. The battery ain’t hooked up. Just don’t cut yourself on those rusty, razor sharp edges.”

Josh hesitated. Because of his large brain. “Do you have any work gloves?”

“Don’t believe in them. Spend good money on gloves, and all they do is get all dirty and torn up.”

That was the whole reason for work gloves, but Josh saw no point in arguing. He found a pile of oily rags next to a space heater and some cans of kerosene, and he used an old hand towel to pick up the spike springs.

“See how they attach to those clips under the gun sight? Those springs are strong, so you gotta use pliers to get them on. To activate them, I used the sensors from an old touch lamp on the triggers. First trigger fires the darts. Second trigger sends the juice.”

“What’s the point of this?” Randall asked.

Josh was also curious. It seemed like a crude, overpowered Taser gun. But what good would that do?

“My bestest buddy, Clevis, had a flying chair accident. I resurrected him from the great beyond using leeches and lightning. Electricity turned him into one of them biters. Makes sense that another jolt would turn him back regular.”

Actually, that didn’t make any sense.

Or did it?

Animals *did* rely on electrophysiology to survive. Cells relied on electrical properties. Science had known that since 1786, when Luigi Galvani made severed frog legs contract with an electrostatic generator. Electricity was still used by health practitioners today. Mr. Einstein had attached spikes and springs to defibrillator pads, which were traditionally used to deliver a countershock to the heart in the case of cardiac dysrhythmias. If being in a zombie-like state was akin to some overall, whole-body dysrhythmia—and in the case of the walking dead, why not?—then maybe the eccentric old man was onto something.

"Does it work?" Josh asked, eyeing the weapon.

Mr. Einstein got teary eyed. "Nope. Just made smoke that smelled like a bad case of swamp ass. I don't think I had enough power. Or I need different capacitors. Or coils. Or something."

Josh began to do some mental calculations. He hadn't thought much about Ohm's Law since third grade, and his teachers thought it more important for him to learn how to color within the lines than waste his time with electrical resistivity and conductivity.

"What's a capacitor?" Randall asked.

Josh gave him a *Do I look like Wikipedia?* stare.

"Amps are the killer," Mr. Einstein said. "That's how the electric chair does you in. So I was thinking more 'long the lines of a super stun gun, with lots of volts. Person can't survive more than a few dozen milliamps, but a quick jolt of two million volts will wake a man up. These biters are outta wack, like a wonky heart. A good zap might restart them normal-like."

"Got paper and a pen?" Josh asked.

"I got a dry erase board," Mr. Einstein said. "Over there."

Einstein pointed with his chin. Josh walked over to a large, white board, covered with scribblings, most of them poorly drawn stick figures with large breasts. He picked up the eraser and wiped it across the board. Nothing erased.

"Did you use a permanent marker on this board?" Josh asked, eying a Sharpie.

"Mistakes were made," Mr. Einstein said.

Josh grabbed the marker, found an empty spot on the board without too many boobs, and then jotted down an equation so complicated it's pointless to reproduce it here because nobody would be smart enough to understand it.

"I need some heavy duty electrical components, and a soldering iron," Josh said.

"What are you going to do?" Randall asked.

Josh put his hands on his hips, and tried to look as cool as possible. "I'm going to save the world."

Once he said it, he didn't feel cool. He felt kinda corny and embarrassed.

After a moment of silence, Mr. Einstein said, "You better hurry up there, Woodrow. We only got four minutes left until my birthday."

CLEVIS

Buried under Wood...

Clevis was having hisself the granddaddy of bad days.

It started off good. He found a dime in a pile of dog poop on Main Street. The cashier at Paco Chang's didn't notice his 10% off coupon had expired last week and accepted it. And Clevis was looking forward to finally getting all of those rocks off his barn roof, that he threw up there, just because.

Then things went downhill. He burned to death in a flying chair accident. Got resurrected as a leech-covered cannibal zombie. Hadn't had more than a single bite of anyone since his leech-covered cannibal zombie transformation. Got stabbed in the back by some woman. Then got trapped under a cord of expertly-chopped firewood.

And now, to top it all off with a big, fat raspberry, it had begun to rain.

When Clevis rated this day later on in his diary, he wouldn't rate it more than two and a half stars out of five.

After extracting himself from the cut logs, he sniffed the air and found the drizzle was interfering with his newly acquired bloodhound abilities.

Knock off another quarter star for that.

Clevis wandered around to the front of the house, listening for someone to munch on, and kept hearing that danged jingling sound.

Took a step, heard *ching-a-ling.*

Stopped, and heard nothing.

Like the jingle was following him around, somehow. Mocking his every move.

He ran, and the jingling got even louder.

Irritating.

Clevis tried the front door. It was locked, of course. He saw a car parked in the gravel driveway, and naturally that was locked too.

He leaned against it, ignoring the jingle sound, and wondered what happened to Lake Niboowin. There was a time when neighbors trusted neighbors, and no one locked up their houses or vehicles.

It was sad in a sad, sad way. Because no one trusted no one these days, Clevis couldn't just walk into someone's home and eat them.

He was pondering on that when his legs were pulled out from under him, and he fell onto his face.

Clevis wondered if the rotation of the earth changed directions, which was something his bestest buddy Einstein said happened on a biweekly basis. And then that man Clevis had been chasing crawled out from underneath the car.

"Those are mine!" the man said, reaching down and pulling the car keys out of Clevis's back with a *jinga-ling* sound.

Jinga-ling!

That's what's been tormenting Clevis for the last hour! He had car keys sticking out of his spine!

The man got into the car, started it, then drove straight into the closed garage door attached to the cabin, busting it up in an expensive way. But Clevis was so giddy to finally figure out what that jingle sound was, he didn't pay the man no mind.

Stabbed in the back with car keys. That was rich. He couldn't wait to tell old Einstein.

In fact, sitting down with his bestest buddy, telling him about the two and a quarter star day he'd had, seemed like the best idea Clevis had in quite some time.

So he went to go do it.

Clevis walked around the house, jumped into the lake, and began to swim toward Einstein's house.

The Zombie Horde Arrives...

All eyes were riveted to the barn clock.

Seven fifty-nine and fifty-eight seconds...

Seven fifty-nine and fifty-nine seconds.

Eight o'clock.

Einstein wasn't sure what he was expecting. Maybe some sort of werewolf-like transformation. Or a sudden, powerful urge to eat people. Or his heart exploding out of his chest and growing spider legs and going on a rampage.

Maybe not that last one so much.

But when the clock struck eight, nothing happened. Not one little thing.

"We sure that time is right?" the taller kid asked. Einstein couldn't remember his name. It was Jerry, or something like that.

"Should be right," Einstein said. "I just put in a new battery in '98."

They all waited for another minute.

"How do you feel?" said the shorter kid. Luther, or something similar.

"My hands are numb. And I can't move my legs."

"We wrapped you in duct tape."

"Oh. Right."

Another minute passed.

"Almost done," said the short kid. He'd been soldering something fierce, and the TCD9 looked even more badass than it did before. But Einstein would never admit that, preferring to appear strong and manly in the eyes of these youths.

"Not bad," he said. "But it needs more sparkle glitter."

No one made any move to add more sparkle glitter.

"We need a power source," Shorty said.

"You can tie into the main," Einstein told him. "Use that live wire dangling from the rafters. Might as well put it to some good use."

"Do you have any way to turn off the main power?" Shorty asked.

"Circuit breaker is in the house. Thought about putting a kill switch in the barn, but it don't make sense. By the time a mishap occurred, it would be too late to cut the power."

"Do you have any flashlights?" the tall one, Tally, asked.

"Young man, I'll have you know that I invented a solar powered flashlight over forty years ago."

"Really? Where is it?"

"Next to the fire canister, to your right. Er, your left. No, it's your right."

Shorty found the solar light on his left. He pressed the button and nothing happened.

"It doesn't work."

"Duh," Einstein said. "It's solar powered. It only works when the sun is out."

The children did not seem duly impressed by Einstein's genius.

"Can the light use batteries?" Tally asked.

"Sure. It takes twenty-eight D cells. Or maybe thirty-eight. I don't recall. Forty years is a long time to remember stuff."

"Do you have any D batteries?" Tally asked.

"Nope, but..." Einstein stopped himself. He almost said his wife, Debs, had two Ds, but that was inappropriate to say around young'uns. "Nope."

Shorty was putting on Einstein's duck hunting waders, which were too big on him and produced a comical effect.

"Josh," Tally said, holding out his hand, "give me the gun."

"It's a TCD9, young man. And why are you wearing my wading boots?"

"They're rubber," he said. "So they'll insulate me from touching the ground. I'll only make one point of contact with the electricity, rather than two, so I won't get shocked."

The tall boy looked dubious.

"Shorty is right," Einstein said. "Because science."

"Okay," Tally said. "But let me do it. Those waders are too big on you."

"Don't they look funny, though?" Einstein said. "Like he got hit with a shrink ray."

Shorty hopped out of the boots, and Tally put them on. Then he positioned himself under the sparking live wire—

—and hesitated.

"You'll be fine," Shorty said.

"Your shorter yet handsomer brother is right. Ain't nothing to fear but fear itself," Einstein said. "And your arteries cooking. I seen that happen. Ugly way to die."

"Your arteries won't cook, Randall. Your biggest worry should be the current stopping your heart—"

Tally cast a frantic look at Shorty.

"—but that isn't going to happen either," Shorty said. "You trust me, right?"

"Yeah. Okay. Let's do this."

Tally reached for the wire—

—and attached the hot end to the butt of the weapon.

No deaths. No explosions. No injuries. Which was always a plus when conducting experiments.

"Now we need to test it," Shorty said. "Shoot it at Mr. Einstein."

Unlike Tally, Einstein didn't trust the short one. "Whoa, now. I'm in no current need of… um… current."

"This won't be lethal," Shorty said. "It'll just hurt. A lot."

Einstein didn't want to be hurt. Especially a lot.

"But I don't feel zombified. Maybe this whole sixty-five year bagpipe thing is wrong. Heck, it may not even be my birthday. I get all of the months ending in *Y* confused."

"It's August," Tally said.

"August? I wasn't born in August. It was an *end in Y* month. Like January. Or one of them other ones. January, maybe."

The boys exchanged a glance.

"Look, we got no idea if this thing is going to work," Einstein said. "None of my ideas ever work. I'm a fraud, boys. A failure. I couldn't even make water if I mixed hydrogen and nitrogen."

"It's hydrogen and oxygen," Shorty said.

"See what I mean? I'm an idjit. I killed my bestest friend today, and then like some kind of redneck Frankenstein I brought him back and unleashed a zombified plague upon the world."

"So to redeem yourself, we should test this on you," Randall said, pointing the weapon.

"I didn't say I feel guilty, son. I said I feel stupid. Redemption is for other, nicer people. I'd prefer to live out my last few hours not being zapped with two billion volts."

"The math says it will work," said Shorty.

"Shorty, you want to trust my life to a bunch of squiggles and symbols invented hundreds of years ago by dead people? What if you shoot me, and I turn into some kind of crazed, kid-eating monster?"

"It'll be fine. You're restrained."

"Maybe it'll give me acid for sweat and it'll eat through this tape."

"I'm willing to take that chance," Tall Kid said.

"How can I make this any clearer?" Einstein used his best authoritative voice. "Do not, under any circumstances, shoot me with The Cannibal Destroyer 9000. If you want to test that thing…"

Einstein made a not so subtle gesture toward his wife, hanging from the rafters.

"Zap Miss Debra?" Shorty asked.

"She's zombified. And, while it was exciting for a wee bit to think that maybe I was about to enter my second bachelorhood, I gotta admit I miss my wife the way she once was. She wasn't perfect, but she wasn't trying to eat me, neither." Einstein tried to summon up a crocodile tear or two, and failed. But he managed to fake a little flutter in his voice. "I love her. For better or for worse. Bring her back to me, boys. Please."

The children looked like they were buying it. Kids were so gullible.

Einstein poured on the syrup. "If I didn't have to put tape on her mouth to keep her from snacking on me, I'm sure Debs would agree. Isn't that right, Debs?"

Debs began to growl and thrash something violent.

"See?" Einstein said. "That means *yes*."

"We do need to test it on a zombie, Josh," Tally said.

Shorty rubbed his chin, then nodded. "Okay. The math works. Do it."

Tally aimed the TCD9 toward Debs—

—and Einstein felt something he'd never felt before.

He wasn't sure what it was. Worry? Guilt?

Love?

Oh, dear lord in heaven, I actually love her.

I love her and I don't want nothin' bad to happen to her.

And if these kids zap her with my stupid TCD9, which I thought up in my stupid head, and it hurts my wife somehow, I'll never forgive myself and miss her so bad that I'll visit her grave every day with fresh flowers and tender love poems that actually rhyme for real, not like that one I wrote where I tried to rhyme marriage *with* cherish.

"Wait!" he yelled. "Shoot me inst—"

And then there was blinding bright light, and a sound of thunder, and everything went black.

Outside of Einstein's Barn...

She gave the barn door a soft tug.

Locked.

Then the lights winked out.

It didn't bother Grandma. Her eyesight was just as good as her hearing.

Inside the barn, Randall said, "Did it work?"

"Can't see nothing," answered Rupert. "Breaker must have tripped."

"Where's the breaker?" Josh asked.

"Inside the house. In the kitchen."

"I'll go," said Randall.

"No," Josh said. "You hold onto the TCD9. I'll be right back. Do you have a candle or something, Mr. Einstein?"

"I melted down all my candles to make an invisible box."

"Did it work?"

"I dunno. I can't find it."

Grandma began to circle the barn, searching for another entrance. She found a window, but it was too tiny for her to crawl through.

"How am I supposed to find the circuit breaker in the dark?" Josh asked.

"I'll go," Rupert said.

"You were bitten. You could change."

"I told you, I was born in March."

"How can somebody forget their own birthday?"

"My brain is crammed full of all this genius inventor stuff. Got no room for nothing else."

"Man…" Randall said. "What's that terrible smell?"

Grandma sniffed. The drizzle made it harder to detect odors, but there was an awful stink coming from inside the barn.

"Sorry," Rupert said. "I break wind when I get nervous."

She shook her head, frowning. That Rupert always was a rude fellow.

"It smells like salami and poor choices," Randall said. "And… is it actually glowing green?"

"Meat stick flashlight," Einstein said. "Hey, you need light? Grab a couple of those mason jars and come over here. I got a gutful of renewable energy."

"You do it, Josh."

"You do it."

"You told me to hold onto the TCD9."

"Fine. I'll go."

Grandma heard movement inside as she prowled the barn's perimeter. The footfalls of a child.

"Okay," Rupert said, "now hold the open jar near my posterior region."

"I think I'd rather go outside and let the zombies eat me," Josh said.

She grinned. *Good idea, Josh. Grandma is waiting for you.*

"Just do it, Josh."

"This is so gross. Okay. Go ahead."

Ten seconds passed.

"What's taking so long?" Randall asked.

"I don't want to push too hard," Rupert said. "That would be bad for everybody."

Ten more seconds ticked by. Grandma finished her lap of the barn. The door was the only way in. She needed something to help her get inside. A big rock, maybe. Or a log she could swing.

Such a shame she hadn't thought to bring her fire axe.

"You know what?" Rupert said. "Debs made bacon and beans tonight. Run into the kitchen, grab me a bowl. That oughta help."

"If I could see in the house, I wouldn't need a jar of glowing farts."

"Good point. Wait… okay… wait… almost… there's my little stink baby. The strong, silent type."

"This one's so big I can feel the heat." Josh gagged. "Lid is on. Tight."

"Damn," Randall said. "That's bright enough to light up the room."

"Talk about your greenhouse gasses," Josh said through his hand, which was pressed over his nose and mouth.

"Breaker panel is in the kitchen, on the wall next to the sink," Rupert said. "Also, bring back that leftover bacon and beans."

"Okay. I'll be right back."

Grandma heard the sound of wood against wood. Then the barn door opened.

Josh zipped past like a lightning bug, leaving a faint phosphorescent trail as he headed for the house.

Grandma considered her options. She could go into the barn and eat Randall and Rupert, but the smell was definitely spoiling her appetite.

She chose to follow Josh.

Fast and silent as a shark, she followed her bite-size grandson into the house.

In Mr. Einstein's Cabin…

Yucky as it was holding a mason jar full of an old guy's air biscuit, the brownish-green glow did allow Josh to see in the dark. He reached Mr. Einstein's front door, hesitating. This whole thing felt weird. The strange house, the dark, the eerie glow. Josh was overcome with an urge to knock and say *Trick or Treat*.

Randall loved Halloween. Josh wasn't a fan. Sure, he liked the candy. And he enjoyed the cosplay (last year he dressed up as Johannes Gutenberg, inventor of the printing press.) But he hated scary movies. Josh still couldn't watch *The Wizard of Oz* because the Wicked Witch freaked him out. He especially hated when people tried to scare him. Like at the Jaycee's Haunted House, where every year you paid ten bucks to walk through an old office building decorated to look like an insane asylum, while stoned teenagers in rubber masks jumped out and said *Boo!* to make you scream.

Josh always screamed. He screamed before they even jumped out. And after this terrible day he'd had, Josh's already nervous disposition was past his endurance limit. Pretend monsters were bad enough. Josh now had to deal with real monsters. And the thought of going into an old, dark, house made his knees knock.

I should go back. Let Randall do this.

He turned, and heard splashing sounds. Coming from the lakeshore.

The zombies.

They're coming.

That harsh slap of reality was enough to motivate Josh. There was no time to trade places with Randall. He needed to get the power back on, and get back to the barn before…

Not pausing to think anymore, Josh turned the doorknob and hurried into Mr. Einstein's house. Holding the fart jar in front of him like Bilbo creeping through Gollum's lair with his glowing sword, Sting (Josh read the books but didn't see the movies—too scary), he made his way through a narrow hallway and into a living room. Josh hadn't known what to expect, but the room was the opposite of Einstein's workshop. It was orderly and clean and tastefully decorated, and the couch looked so comfy it reminded Josh how tired he was.

He made his way into the next room, a dining area, with a large, rectangular table surrounded by six ornate chairs. A china cabinet dominated one wall, filled with ceramic pieces, dozens of scented candles, and various pictures of Mr. Einstein and Miss Debra in their younger years.

CREAK.

Josh turned toward the sound, coming from behind, knowing instantly what it was.

The front door closing—

—and locking.

Rooted to the spot, Josh was unsure what to do. Someone, or something, was in the house with him.

Randall, maybe?

Randall would have called to him.

Run?

Hide?

Hiding seemed best. He set the glowing jar on the table, then crouched down, crawling to the breakfront. It had cabinet doors on the lower section, and Josh opened one—

—staring straight into a pair of dead, black eyes.

Josh slapped his hands over his mouth so he didn't scream. The eyes belonged to a large, and terrifying, child's doll. One of the old ones with celluloid skin and curly mohair, that stood a meter tall and had that creepy, uncanny valley look.

Josh pushed the doll to the side and crawled in next to her. Cinnamon and vanilla—from the many scented candles in the cabinet—assaulted his nostrils. Josh sat down, pulling his legs inside. It was a tight squeeze, and couldn't fully shut the cabinet door, because it didn't have a handle on the inside. So he got it as closed as he could.

"I know you're here, Josh," a familiar voice cooed.

Josh froze, terror enveloping him like a shroud.

Oh, no. It's Grandma.

"Remember all the bedtime stories I used to read to you?"

She sounded muffled, far away. Probably in the hall.

Please don't let her come any closer.

"What was your favorite story? Mine was always *Little Red Riding Hood.*"

Her footsteps drew nearer. She was in the living room.

"Why, Grandma," she said, using Red Riding Hood's voice. "What big ears you have." Then she lowered it to play the wolf. "All the better to hear you with, my dear."

Josh hugged his knees. A tiny line of green light peeked through the crack in the cabinet door, and he could see a sliver of carpet.

Don't come in here. Don't come in here.

"Why, Grandma, what a big nose you have. All the better to sniff you with, my dear." Grandma snorted. "And you smell like goulash simmering in a slow cooker."

A floorboard creaked in the dining room. She was really close now. Josh bit his lower lip so he didn't whimper, and he held his breath.

"Why, Grandma, what sharp teeth you have..."

The footsteps stopped.

"You know that the next line is, don't you, baby?"

Don't let her find me.

Josh squeezed his eyes shut, determined not to make any noise. He knew, from his horrible underwater experience, that he could hold his breath for at least a minute. If he didn't breathe, she couldn't hear him.

And hopefully she couldn't smell him in the cabinet, because it was filled with so many scented candles.

"It's rude not to answer your Grandma, Josh."

Josh peeked. He could see Grandma's shoe, through the crack in the door. She was *right there*. Standing directly in front of him.

"Red Riding Hood says, 'Why, Grandma, what sharp teeth you have.' And what does Grandma say?"

Please don't let her find me.

Please don't let her find me.

Please don't let her find me.

Please don't—

The cabinet door opened.

"All the better to eat you with," Grandma said.

Josh screamed. Then he screamed again when he saw her dentures.

Each of Grandma's teeth had been filed to a sharp point, giving her a mouthful of fangs.

In Mr. Einstein's Barn...

The barn was glowing pretty good, and I had my shirt stretched up over my nose and was breathing through that to try and limit the stench.

It didn't help much.

"I think we have enough light," I said.

"The meat stick flashlight is a helpful, but ultimately cruel, invention," Mr. Einstein said. "A lot of folks prefer to just remain in the dark when it comes to new technology. But reality always finds you. Can't hide from the truth. Even if it stinks. If you're a loser, you'll ultimately be confronted with your failures."

He sniffled.

"Don't cry, Mr. Einstein. Maybe she's okay."

"She's just hanging there, limp-like. I never should have let Wesley shoot her with that gosh-darn, confound-it TCD9. My inventions never work. You know I once made a robot that could tie your shoes? Named him Friendly. Know what Friendly did?"

"Tied your shoes?"

"Friendly went on a killing spree."

I couldn't believe it. "It actually killed people?"

"Tried to. Chased me all through the house, screaming like something straight outta hell, tying knots in damn near everything in its path. I hacked Friendly to pieces with my trusty kitchen axe, which I keep in the kitchen, next to the circuit breaker. Every home should have a kitchen axe, I always say. Actually, that's the first time I ever said that. Maybe I should write it down so I don't forget." He let out a booming wail. "Oh, Debs! I'm such an idiot!"

I didn't argue. Instead he said, "Shh."

"I know, a grown man shouldn't cry like this. On top of a dumb failure, I'm a shameful embarrassment. Debs, I'm sorry for everything! When I see you again in the afterlife I promise I'll never make no bad comments about your terrible cooking ever again!"

"Mr. Einstein, keep it down. I think I hear something."

There was noise, outside the barn. Coming from the lake.

Splashing.

And moaning.

"They're here," I said.

"Who? Has Friendly come back with a squad of robot killers?" Mr. Einstein's eyes became the size of dinner plates. "They warned us artificial intelligence would destroy the world! But we geniuses had to play God!"

"It's the zombies!" I said, letting the TCD9 hang by its wire and clodhopping to the barn door in the rubber waders. As soon as I stuck my head outside, one of the geriatric undead took a swipe at me. And he was just one of a whole bunch, treading up the shore, heading for us.

"Shut the door, Spanky!"

I grabbed the barn door—

—and hesitated.

Josh was still in Mr. Einstein's house. If I locked the barn, how could he get back in?

"My brother—"

"He'll be safe! Lock that door or we're all gonna be zombie snacks!"

More of the living dead were coming around the barn, from the other direction. Lightning flashed, giving me a brief glimpse of the whole yard as the thunder rocked the earth.

There were over a hundred zombies, and at least ten between me and the house.

I had seconds to make a decision.

Mosh my way through the zombie horde to try and get to Josh, leaving Mr. Einstein to be eaten? Or shut the door and try to fend off the end of the world while coming up with some sort of plan?

That's when I heard Josh scream.

I had to go for it. I braced myself to run the gauntlet.

"There's a tunnel!" Mr. Einstein yelled. "Between the house and the barn!"

I turned to look at him.

"A tunnel?"

"Shut the damn door!"

Zombies rushing at me from six directions at once, I closed the barn door and slammed the lock into place.

Then the pounding began. Not just at the door, but the walls, too. Pounding and wailing, until the entire barn was surrounded by monsters trying to break in.

It was some real *Night Of The Living Dead* shit.

I hurried over to Mr. Einstein. "Where's the tunnel?"

He met my eyes. "Untape me."

"Tell me where the tunnel is, you stinky old redneck!"

Mr. Einstein seemed incredibly calm, considering the situation. "Listen, Maurice. I can help you. Even if you use the tunnel, those things are gonna get into the house. You'll need me to fight at your side. It's the only way to save little Stimey."

I wasn't sure what to do. Kicking him came to mind, but I wasn't the type to hurt anyone. Especially when they were tied up.

"Look," he said in soothing tones, "you can see I'm not a zombie, can't you?"

"I dunno. It's hard to see in here."

Mr. Einstein ripped one that sounded like a chainsaw starting. I covered my nose and mouth.

"Do I look like one of them creatures?"

The greenish-brown glow surrounded him. The stench was making my eyes water. I held my nose and shook my head.

"That's because I ain't a zombie. Get me free. We'll figure this out together. I promise."

He seemed sincere. I considered my choices, but I didn't really have any. So I found some rusty garden shears and spent a few minutes freeing him.

"Okay, where's the tunnel?" I asked, pointing the shears at him in case he tried something.

"Ain't no tunnel."

"You said there was a tunnel."

He shrugged. "I fibbed."

I tried to process what he said, but was having trouble connecting the dots.

"So how do we save Josh?"

"There is no *we*," Mr. Einstein said.

"But you told me—"

"I lie. All the time. About everything. On top of that, I'm a coward. If you want to try to save him, you're on your own. But you'll have to find some way to pass through solid wood, because there is no way I'm letting you open that door."

"But my brother—"

"You keep going on and on about your brother. Your brother has most certainly been half-digested by now. Can't grieve forever. I've gotten over my dearly departed Debs. Been five minutes, and she'd want me to move on. I'm already composing my Match.com personal ad in my head. *Recent widower with rugged good looks and genius brain seeks millionaire exotic dancer. Good cooks a plus.*"

I was trying to figure out what to do next when there was a rattling sound from above, louder than the horde trying to break in.

Chains.

We both looked up.

"Debs? That you, Debs? You okay?"

Mr. Einstein reached for a switch on the wall, flipping it up.

Nothing happened.

"Crapballs. Out of gas." He looked at me. "I need you to climb those rafters and hit the release pin on that gear."

Well, this was an interesting development.

"Just put in more gas," I said.

"How the heck am I supposed to get way up there?"

"How did you fill it up in the first place?"

"I winched myself up."

"So use a ladder." I folded my arms across my chest. "You have a ladder, don't you?"

"A'course I got a ladder!"

"Where is it?"

"I took it apart and used the pieces."

"For what?"

"To make the winch."

I was beginning to realize that most of the conversations with Mr. Einstein were circular in nature. It didn't matter. I finally had some bargaining power.

"If I help get her down, will you help me save my brother?"

"You have my word."

"You just told me you lie all the time."

"Well, dang it, what do you want me to do? Sign a contract? Swear on a bible?"

Not the worst idea ever. "Do you have a bible?"

"No." Mr. Einstein looked around and picked something up off the floor. "I got this takeout menu from the *Cracker Barrel*."

Overhead, Miss Debra moaned. I knew I was going to help, regardless of how big a jerk Mr. Einstein was. It was the right thing to do. Plus, this was the only way to know if Josh's souped-up TCD9 actually worked.

"Fine. Raise your right hand and repeat after me."

Mr. Einstein raised his left hand. I figured it was close enough.

"I…"

"I."

"Your name."

Mr. Einstein's face crinkled up. "I can't remember your name. I don't have a good memory for names. Or facts. Or knowledge. What are you called? Dutch? Meadowlark? Hambone?"

"Randall."

"Gotcha." He cleared his throat. "I, Randall."

I rubbed my eyes. "Just say you swear you'll help my brother."

"I swear. Now please get my Debs down."

I took off the rubber waders and squinted up at the ceiling, dust and bits of dirt raining down as the undead mob pounded on the walls, rattling the barn to the foundation. The motes in the air reflected Mr. Einstein's glowfarts (I'm going to trademark that word), making it bright enough for me to see a good route. There were X beams bracing the sides of the barn. I could shimmy up one of those, then go hand-over-hand across the rafters to the winch gear.

In theory, anyway. I was about to see if it was as easy as it looked.

I turned back to Mr. Einstein, to ask for a boost, but he was engrossed in a tattered old *Jughead & Archie Digest*. So I began to climb without assistance.

At first, it was easy. I had good handholds, my shoes were gripping well, and I ascended eight feet in just as many seconds. No harder than going up a ladder, or a tree, and much easier than the climbing wall at the YMCA.

But on this day, nothing wound up being easy.

Halfway up the X beam, I gripped an old RC Cola tin sign to take a brief rest, and the sign bent in half, causing me to lose my footing.

For a moment I dangled there by one hand, my whole body tingling with fear, my heart practically jumping out of my throat and slapping me for my poor judgment. I scrambled fast to get my feet back on wood, and managed to find a toehold without falling.

"Jumpin' Jethro with a hotfoot, be careful!" Mr. Einstein shouted up at me. "I paid twelve dollars for that sign!"

Then he went back to Jughead.

The second half of the X went a bit slower, because; height. From the ground, a sixteen foot ceiling didn't seem like much. But looking down, the distance was almost paralyzing. If I fell, I'd be lucky to escape with only a broken leg or two. Paralyzation, maiming, and death were more likely. Many of Mr. Einstein's piles of junk contained sharp stuff. He even had a large crate marked *sharp stuff,* not too far away from where Miss Debra was hanging.

"Don't do it!" I heard Mr. Einstein yell.

I glanced at him, waiting for more. But his nose was still buried in the comic.

"You'll never eat that whole birthday cake, Jughead! It's a surefire tummy ache!"

Miss Debra was five rafters away, wiggling and squirming in a way that gave no clear indication she was either human or monster. The overhead boards were two-by-fours, and I tested the closest to me by gripping it tight and letting it hold my weight.

Seemed sturdy enough.

Outside, a clap of thunder momentarily drowned out the rioting undead trying to bust their way in. I fixed my eyes on the big gear, next to the outboard motor crudely clamped to the main beam, and then began to muscle my way across, from one rafter to the next, like they were monkey bars on a playground.

The world's suckiest playground.

Four to go…

Three…

Two…

"Silly Jughead! Now you're gonna be sick as a dog!"

One!

Then the rafter cracked and bowed.

My life didn't flash before my eyes. I didn't have any profound insights, or final thoughts, or fear of death. I just felt a pang of regret that I wasn't there for Josh.

But I didn't fall. The cracked rafter didn't break in half. It held me just fine.

"What you waitin' on, boy? Stop playin' around and hit the gear release!"

I gave Mr. Einstein a look, and he was lucky I didn't have laser vision because I would have fried his giblets. When my irritation abated, I carefully stretched out my hand and pressed the lever.

Miss Debra plummeted—

—right into Mr. Einstein's arms.

"Welcome back, baby. I knew I'd be able to rescue you."

I stared as Mr. Einstein tore the strip of duct tape off of Miss Debra's mouth—

—and she snarled and bit him on the face.

In Mr. Einstein's Cabin…

Grandma lunged, and Josh pushed the antique doll into her clawed hands, simultaneously ducking between her legs. Then he hauled butt out of the dining area and into the next room.

The kitchen!

The glowfart jar (Josh decided to have that word copyrighted) barely illuminated that far, but it threw enough shadows for Josh to see the outline of the sink. He ran to it, frantically feeling along the wall.

There! A panel!

A millisecond later he was flipping the main circuit breaker switch.

Let there be light…

Josh ran right past the refrigerator (even though he told Mr. Einstein otherwise, Josh had no intention of bringing back the bacon and beans. Mr. Einstein needed beans like a firefighter needed lighter fluid.) Then he headed for the doorway, assuming it looped back into the hall, and began to sprint—

—only to be blocked by Grandma.

Josh slid on the linoleum, falling onto his butt, and then crab-walked backwards, bumping into something that was leaning against the wall. It fell in front of him, clattering to the floor.

A mop? A broom?

Mr. Einstein's kitchen axe! Every home should have one!

Josh scooped it up and stood on shaky legs.

"I don't want to hurt you," he said, slowly backing away.

Grandma advanced. "I don't want to hurt you either, baby. I just want to eat you."

Josh made a lame swing with the axe, sticking it into the floor. Grandma pounced on it, yanking the axe away from Josh with ease.

"Hasn't Grandma taught you anything?" she said, smiling wide with those horrible fangs. "Here's the proper way to swing an axe."

She raised it above her head—

—and got it stuck on the overhead track lighting.

Josh didn't pause to dwell on the happy fact that he wasn't cleaved in half. He dashed past Grandma as she struggled to free the axe, and then darted out the front door and into a herd of zombies.

It was like something straight out of a cheezy horror novel.

The rain was really starting to come down. Josh slid to a stop on the wet grass, bracing himself for the mob to turn on him.

But they didn't. They continued to pound and beat on the barn.

They can't smell me.

His relief was short-lived when he realized he would be soaking wet very soon and had no idea where to go. The barn door was closed, no doubt locked. If it had been a warm day rather than a cold, rainy night, Josh would have taken off into the woods, preferring getting lost to being eaten. But he'd already begun to shiver. Josh didn't have much body mass, and quickly calculated that hypothermia would immobilize him within fifteen minutes.

Go around the house. Find another way in. Wait for Randall.

Hiding hadn't worked with Grandma. But maybe he could barricade himself in a room, or climb up into the crawlspace. He walked quickly, not wanting to draw attention to himself, and then noticed the window on the barn.

The zombies weren't bothering with it, because it was too small for them to fit through.

But Josh could fit through it.

So… the house? Or the barn?

The zombies were banging on the barn pretty hard, and didn't seem to be making any headway breaking into it. It seemed pretty safe. Plus, the TCD9 was inside, and the power was back on. Josh was sure his math was sound. If he was right, they could stop Armageddon.

Josh hurried to the window. When he got there, he realized it was too high for him to reach.

"It's one of the boys!" someone shouted.

Josh turned. The zombies had discovered him.

And he had nowhere to run.

In The Barn...

I just hung there, watching in horror as Miss Debra chewed on Mr. Einstein's face.

Then I realized that she wasn't eating him.

She was kissing him. With a whole lot of tongue.

I just hung there, watching in horror as two old people made out. Then I heard my little brother yell.

"Randall! Help! I'm by the window!"

I changed my grip, quickly turning around, and then went hand-over-hand, back to the wall.

"Josh is outside!" I cried to Mr. Einstein.

"Who?"

"My brother! You promised to help!"

He snorted. "Or else, what? I can't eat at the Cracker Barrel no more?"

Miss Debra gave him a rough punch in the shoulder. "You promised him, Rupert! Now go save that boy!"

Mr. Einstein went sheepish and said, "Yes, dear."

As I made my way down the wall, Mr. Einstein opened up the tiny window and reached a hand outside.

"Come on, Homer! Ain't got all day!"

I knew this wouldn't turn out well, because that was just the way this day was going. Mr. Einstein would pull a zombie inside instead of Josh. Or he'd start screaming, and when he brought his arm back all the flesh would be eaten off. Or something else equally horrible would happen. I would have bet my allowance for the rest of my life that there was no way in hell—

"Got him," Mr. Einstein said, yanking Josh safely inside and setting him down.

So much for my predictions.

I made it to ground level, and gave Josh the biggest hug ever.

"Yuck, Randall," he said, squirming.

"I'm just so happy to see you, little bro."

"Not that. Over there."

He pointed at Einstein, who was groping Miss Debra inappropriately. And she was groping him back, even worse.

I mean, c'mon. There were children present. And a zombie apocalypse outside. Pick a better time.

"I didn't think the elderly did that," Josh said.

Mr. Einstein stopped pawing his wife long enough to sneer at us. "You kids think sexy is what you see in *Tiger Beat Magazine* and on *Soul Train* TV. But beauty ain't all bell bottom pants and platform shoes."

"What decade does he think this is?" Josh asked.

"Sexy is a state of mind," said Mr. Einstein. "Now I want you kids to turn around while Mr. Einstein takes a spunky pill, and don't look again for two to three minutes."

Josh and I didn't question it. We immediately turned around.

That's when the axe came through the barn door.

"Forgot to mention," Josh said as we backed away. "Grandma found the kitchen axe."

"Every household should have one," I muttered, looking around for a weapon for what seemed like the hundredth time in the last five hours.

Grandma, true to her firefighting roots, was getting through that door pretty quick. Thinking of her job as a firefighter sparked some recent memory, and I recalled that fire canister I'd seen somewhere in the barn.

There! Next to the solar powered flashlight.

I snatched it up, looking for the pin you were supposed to pull. It wasn't there. So I tested it by squirting it at a pile of oily rags.

Six feet of flame shot out of the nozzle, and the rags went up like… well… oily rags.

"You idjit!" Mr. Einstein screeched. "Why'd you go and do that?!"

"I… I… I thought it was a fire extinguisher," I stammered. "It says *fire* on the side."

Einstein took the canister away from me. "It says *fire* 'cause that's what it sprays! Fire! I got a can that says *poison* over there, why don't you just go and spray it in my face?"

The flames spread incredibly fast, firetrap that the barn was.

Grandma was just as fast with her axe, breaking through the barn door and standing before us, bits of chopped wood around her feet.

"Quick, Debs!" Mr. Einstein bellowed. "Hide behind this barrel of kerosene with me!"

They disappeared into the smoke. Leaving Josh and me to face Grandma alone.

"Get the TCD9," I said to Josh.

"Where are the rubber boots?" he asked, his voice shaky.

I searched for them. They were next to the wall—

—on fire and half-melted.

Grandma approached us, raising the axe. In the flickering flames, I saw her teeth had been sharpened.

We were dead.

After all the struggling, all the effort, it had come to this. Josh and I had been chased, hurt, terrified, near-drowned, bitten, and almost killed too many times to count.

I wasn't going to learn to drive a car. I wasn't going to lose my virginity. I wasn't even going to live to see another sunrise.

This was it. Game over. Josh and I had tried our hardest, but it hadn't been enough.

We never had a chance.

I looked down at my little brother, shivering and frightened, and I knew what I had to do.

"Hold on, Grandma," I told her, raising my palm up. "You win. I won't fight you anymore."

Grandma halted.

"You can have me," I said. "No struggle. No trying to escape. But please… I beg you…" The tears began to flow down my face. "Let Josh go."

"Randall, no!" Josh said.

"It's okay, bro. It has to be this way."

"No, it doesn't!" he said, stomping his little foot. "Eat me, Grandma. Let Randall go."

"Don't listen to him," I implored. "He's just a kid."

"You're a kid too, Randall!" Josh began to sob. "Don't you do this! Don't you leave me alone!"

I stepped in front of Josh, and stared hard at the monster that was once my Grandma, stared straight into her milky, undead eyes, and I offered my hand.

"Take me, spare Josh," I said. "Do we have a deal?"

BARBARA

At Grandma's Cabin…

There was a huge *CRASH!* and the whole house shook.

Barb shouted for her husband, got no reply, and then limped into the hallway, passing the old rotary phone on the wall. Then she stopped and looked at it.

Does this thing even work?

The phone had come with the cabin, when her mother bought the place right after Randall was born, and left it hanging there because it looked quaint. Barbara hadn't ever used one before. While she was old enough to remember a time when no one owned phones (you had to rent them, monthly, from the phone company), the ones in her house growing up were push button. She picked up the receiver, surprised by how heavy it was, and held it to her ear.

A dial tone!

Putting her finger in the dial over the number 9, she turned it until reaching the finger stop, then watched as the dial went back to its original position. Then she dialed a 1, followed by another 1.

It rang.

And rang.

And—

"911, what's your emergency?"

Barbara was so surprised to get through that she almost dropped the receiver.

"I'm on Lake Niboowin. There's a..."

She paused. They wouldn't believe her if she told the truth. But if she soft-pedalled the situation, emergency services would be unprepared when they arrived, and possibly hurt or killed.

"I think it's terrorists," Barb said. "I don't know how many. But there's one in my house, in the kitchen. He tried to..." she almost said *he tried to eat me*. "He tried to kill me."

"Are you hurt?"

"Yes. And they have my kids, and I can't find my husband." Barbara looked down the hallway, toward the garage. That's where the crash sound had most likely come from. Was Tom in the garage?

Or something else?

"What's your name?"

"My name is—"

And then the phone was ripped out of the wall. Barb spun around, staring in horror as Gustav dropped it onto the floor.

"Terrorists?" the zombie said. "Really? We're just a disenfranchised minority, trying to recoup the respect we've earned. We're not spreading terror to further some ideology. We're just... *hungry*."

Gustav opened his mouth, Barbara bashed him in the chops with the receiver. His uppers cracked in half and fell out of his mouth. He seemed extraordinarily saddened by it.

"I don't think Poligrip can fix—"

She smacked him again, knocking out his lowers and kicking them across the floor. He trudged after them, and Barbara headed for the garage—

—stopping as it opened.

"Tom!"

He ran to her, and they embraced.

"You okay?" he said

She nodded, her face buried in his shoulder. "The boys are on the lake."

"Your mother has a paddleboat. We'll find them."

Tom took her hand and led her back through the garage, grabbing an electric lantern hanging on the tool rack and giving it to her. He also grabbed two rain ponchos, with hoods, and they put them on. Then Tom picked up a crowbar; one of the heavy-duty firefighting models used for breaching.

"Ready?" he asked.

She nodded. The pain in her belly was bad, but being reunited with her husband had given her an energy boost.

"Let's not split up again," she said.

Tom's face softened. "Babe, when this is over, I'm not letting you, or the kids, out of my sight ever again."

He held her chin and gave Barbara an all-too-quick peck on the lips.

Together, they walked around their car, which had part of the garage door embedded in the front windshield.

"I'll tell you later," he said.

Barbara turned on the lantern, and the couple walked through the rain. making their way to the shoreline. The Fiberglas paddleboat was on its side, resting against a tree. Tom pushed it right-side up, then dragged it down the beach, to the water. He pulled it into knee-deep water, and helped Barbara into one of the two seats.

"Tom!"

She pointed across the lake, at a huge fire.

"It's them," Barbara said.

Call it intuition, or motherly instinct, but she knew that's where her boys were.

They put their feet on the bicycle-style pedals.

"If we go fast, we can be there in under five minutes," Tom said.

They peddled as fast as they could.

In Rupert's Barn...

The hunger was all-consuming. It was all she could think about. Ever since the Change, ninety-nine percent of her brain was focused on eating and eating and eating. She'd never felt so hungry. She'd never felt so needy. Nothing in her life had ever been as powerful as her desire for devouring human flesh.

But one percent of Grandma was still human. And that one percent looked at her grandchildren, her brave little boys, whose diapers she'd changed and boo-boos she'd kissed. Who'd eaten thousands of her cookies. Who'd listened to hundreds of bedtime stories. Whom she would have died for, thousands of times over, just to make sure they were safe.

And now they stood before her. Not babies anymore. But young adults. Their whole lives ahead of them. Acting so brave. Being so selfless.

And something inside her broke.

She was so proud of her grandchildren.

She *loved* her grandchildren.

That one percent inside her that was still human pushed back against that terrible hunger. Her insides twisted in agony, and her mind howled in rage, but she was NOT going to eat these precious kids.

And heaven help anyone who tried to harm them in any way.

Grandma dropped the axe, spit her dentures onto the floor, and forced a smile.

"I'll protect you, boys. Your grandma will protect you."

Then she turned to face the mob of undead pouring into the barn.

"What are you fools doing just standing there!" she shouted. "Do you want to eat these children raw, or well-done?"

There was some back-and-forth in the crowd, and the majority answered, "Raw."

"Then grab those buckets over there!" Grandma ordered. "Form a line back to the lake. We need to put out this fire before the whole place burns down!"

All the zombies stood there, staring blankly.

"MOVE YOUR ASSES!" she bellowed.

They did, and the makeshift brigade was formed, splashing bucket after bucket of lake water onto the flames. And they were getting the job done, too.

Old-fashioned did not equal irrelevant.

"They're distracted," Grandma told her kids. "I'll make sure you can get away."

"We can change them back to normal, Grandma," said little Josh. "We can change you back."

"How?"

"That gun, hanging there from the sparking wire. If we zap the zombies, the rain and wet ground will conduct the electricity. We just need something rubber to stand on. Whoever shoots the gun needs to be insulated, or…"

"Or what?" Grandma asked.

"I'm not sure. Without being grounded or insulated, whoever shoots it could cook. Or their heart could burst. Or their whole body could explode."

Randall looked at his younger brother. "You didn't mention the *whole body exploding* thing when I did it."

"You had the rubber waders on. You were fine."

"What in the heck are you doing? Are you plotting something with your grandkids?"

Grandma recognized that irritating voice. She swiveled around and saw Mildred Kanipple, hands on her hips, standing in the doorway.

"Buzz off, Mildred." Grandma had been waiting decades to say that to her.

But Mildred didn't buzz off. "I will admit that I've been known, now and again, to eavesdrop."

That was the understatement of the century. Mildred was the queen of hearsay, and the biggest gossip in four counties.

"Go eavesdrop elsewhere," Grandma said.

"Well, it's a good thing I'm not doing that," Mildred said, raising her voice, "because this woman doesn't want to eat these tasty young men! She's trying to protect them!"

The bucket brigade stopped.

"Mind your business, Mildred Kanipple," Grandma said, pointing a finger. "Unless you want trouble."

Mildred snorted. "What trouble? I've beaten you six years straight in the bake-off. You're strictly runner-up material. A runner-up in baking. And a runner-up in life."

Grandma made a fist. "Really? What would you say if I told you that this runner-up is about to knock that smug right off of your face? You know I could."

"I'll admit that. A lady such as myself would never engage in fisticuffs with an uncultured brute like you. But I ain't the only one here that wants a bite of your grandkids. What are you going to do? Beat us all up?"

Grandma stood in front of Josh and Randall, and planted her feet. "If it comes to that. But you'll be first. We'll see if you can make a flaky pie crust with both your arms in casts."

"Just the kind of violent threat I'd expect from a former firefighter."

"A former *fire chief*," Grandma corrected. "Now are you gonna make a move? Or is your plan to bore me to death with your non-stop yapping?"

Mildred Kanipple hesitated. And for a moment, Grandma thought she won the standoff. She was just about to order everyone to get back to the bucket brigade, and then saw Mildred's eyes go squinty with resolve.

"Get her!" Mildred screeched.

Then everybody rushed into the barn.

In the Barn…

The flames surrounded them, a wall of fire high as the ceiling.

"I told you this place was a fire hazard," Debs said to Einstein.

"You were right, dear. You're right about everything."

"You mean that?"

"I do."

His wife snuggled against him, giving him a peck on the cheek. "Sorry I gnawed on you, Rupert. I know we quarrel a lot. But I do love you."

"I love you, too. That's why I'm going to figure out how to save us."

Einstein racked his genius brain. There had to be some way to escape. Surely one of the hundreds of things he'd invented over the decades could help them.

If only we could fly out of here.

Fly? Wait a dadgum second…

The flying chair!

Clevis had burned the one he'd made earlier, but Einstein had a spare parachute, and the fire canister, and lawn chairs aplenty. It wouldn't take more than a minute or two to make a new one. All he had to do was slap it together, open up the hatch in the roof, and he and Debs could fly to safety.

"See that green button over there?" he pointed. "As I'm constructing our escape vehicle, I need you to press it in a certain sequence to open the roof. Ready?"

Debs nodded, touching the button.

"Tap it long, short short. Short. Long, short, short, short. Short, short, short."

His wife made a face. "What kind of foolishness is that?"

"It's Morse code," Einstein said. "So no one can open it without my permission."

"Morse code?"

"Morse code for *Debs*."

Debs batted her eyelashes and touched her heart. "Aww, really? You old sweetie, you. Tell it to me again."

"It's Morse code for Debs."

"Tell me the sequence, Rupert."

"Oh. Right."

He gave it to her while duct taping the parachute to the lawn chair. Eyeballing his wife, he guessed her weight and reinforced the tape with another layer. The flames were getting dangerously close now. So close Einstein felt like he'd jumped into a pre-heating oven.

"It didn't work," Debs said.

"Lemme try."

Einstein tapped out the proper order of dashes and dots, but the roof hatch stayed closed. It didn't make sense. The power was on.

He squinted up at the ceiling, peering through the gathering smoke, and saw the problem. When that boy, Jeremy, had released the winch gear, the chain whipped up and got stuck in the hatch hinge.

"It's jammed," he said.

"I figured out that much. How do we get it unjammed?"

Einstein picked up his boomerang hammer. "Kiss it for good luck, Debs."

She gave it a big, wet smack.

Einstein took careful aim—

—threw it hard—

—missed—

—and the hammer returned and hit him in the back of the head.

Einstein lost consciousness for what couldn't have been more than a few seconds, and when he opened his eyes his wife was kneeling next to him, holding his hand.

"You tried your best, Rupert. I suppose, that's all a gal can ask."

Einstein tried to choke back a tear, but it escaped before he could. "This is especially painful for me, because besides losing my own life and depriving the world of one of its greatest scientific minds, I'm also losing the two people I love most. My wife, and my bestest friend."

"Do you mean that?"

"I do, Debs."

Her eyes got all wet and shiny. "Then kiss us both goodbye… Einstein."

It was the first time Debs had ever called him by his preferred nickname without it sounding like an insult. He craned his neck up to meet her lips.

"I thought I was your bestest friend."

Wait. Was that…?

"Clevis?" Einstein dodged his wife's kiss and saw his bestest buddy, Clevis, sticking his head through the tiny barn window. "Clevis! My bestest buddy in the whole world!"

"Hey!" Debs said, interruptin' all rude-like.

"Whatcha doing, Einstein?" Clevis asked. "Having a bar-b-que?"

"I'm gonna burn to death, buddy."

Clevis shook his head sadly. "Turble way to go. Hurts something fierce. You should try to not let that happen."

"We're trapped in here," Einstein explained to his slow-witted compadre. "I was going to escape using my genius flying chair, but the roof hatch is stuck."

"Don't it have a safety release?"

"It does. But that's on the roof."

"You got a code so people can't open it and get in, but your safety release is on the roof?" Debs said.

Einstein scratched his face. "When you say it like that, it makes me sound stupid."

"If the shoe fits, Rupert."

"Just like a woman. Talking about shoes while we're facing our imminent demise."

Clevis pulled his back outside and stared up into the falling rain. "I can see the safety release from here. So close I bet I could hit it with a rock."

"Shush, Clevis. I'm trying to formulate a plan."

"Sorry, Einstein. Just saying I could hit the safety release with a—"

"I heard you, Clevis. Not let me think for a second. My mind is recalling something from earlier today that might have had foreshadowed this particular situation. Something to do with the flying chair. Wait a chicken-plucking minute… why did I invent the flying chair?"

"To help me get the rocks off my roof, that I threw up there. I'm good at throwing rocks, Einstein."

"I know you are, Clevis. But you have to shut up while I think."

"I'm so done with you," Debs said.

"Now isn't the time, Debs. I'm problem-solving."

"For heaven's sake, Rupert. How much more obvious can it be? Tell your stupid friend to—"

"I got it!" Einstein declared, talking over his wife. "Clevis! Throw a rock at the safety release!"

Clevis's white eyes got wide. "That's genius!"

"I know! Now go and get to it, bestest buddy!"

Debs said, "I want a divorce."

"Shush, now. That's the fear talking. Now come sit on my lap and hold on tight. Soon as Clevis gets that hatch open, ol' Einstein is gonna take his girl on the ride of her life."

Einstein sat in the lawn chair, and Debs plopped down on top of him, making him wonder if he'd used enough duct tape.

"I don't know everything that happened tonight," Debs said. "But I'd bet my last dollar that this is all somehow your fault."

"I admit nothing," Einstein said.

Debs stuck a finger in his face. "I knew it! That's what you always say when you done something stupid."

The flames were close to engulfing them. Einstein held the parachute in one hand, his fire canister in the other.

Now it was all up to Clevis.

Einstein crossed his thumbs and waited for his bestest buddy to come through.

CLEVIS

Outside Einstein's Barn...

Clevis looked around for a rock to throw at the safety release on the roof. He found one, but it was too tiny. He threw it up there anyway, as was his compulsion.

It didn't do nothin'.

As he searched around for a more suitable rock, Clevis's stomach grumbled so hard it felt like he'd eaten a two stroke engine. He couldn't remember ever being so hungry.

That made him think of that nice, young couple, who smelled so delicious. He'd gotten a few bites in, and the taste had been as good as his secret stash of cough drops, that he hid from his wife under the floorboards.

Uh-oh. His wife.

Clevis had been gone all day. His wife would be mad. Probably thought he'd wasted the day, drinkin' beer with Einstein. He could imagine what she'd say.

"You wasted the day, drinkin' beer with Einstein."

And how was he supposed to defend himself? Tell her he didn't have a drop of beer, but instead he got all burned up, came back from the dead, and went on a people-eating spree? That sounded a mite bit worse than wasting the day, drinking beer.

Maybe he could sneak into the house when she was asleep, and in the morning she'd forget about it.

Yeah, that's what he'd do.

Clevis wiped the rain off his head, and began to head home. He had some nagging thought in his noggin that he was supposed to do something important, but he decided not to dwell on it. Clevis forgot stuff all the time.

He'd think of it later. How important could it be, anyway?

In Mr. Einstein's Barn…

An avalanche of geriatric zombies tumbled in the barn.

Grandma punched Mildred Kanipple square in the jaw, knocking her down, then managed to take out four others before she was swallowed by the horde.

Randall led Josh away, deeper inside the burning barn, closer to the TCD9.

Josh knew what his brother had in mind.

He pulled against his brother, trying to keep him away from the gun. "You can't, Randall."

"I'm ending this, Josh."

"If you fire it, you'll fry."

"Maybe your calculations are wrong."

"It isn't my calculations, Randall. It's Ohm's law."

"Maybe Ohm is wrong."

"Ohm isn't wrong!"

Josh began to cry. Less than a minute ago, they'd gotten their Grandma back. She'd fought whatever had control over her body, and Josh had believed everything was going to work out okay.

Now Grandma was being trampled, and Randall was once again trying to sacrifice himself to save the world.

Randall shook off Josh's grip, then reached for the TCD9—

—taking it in both hands.

"See?" Randall said above the zombie moans and crackling flames. "Didn't shock me."

"It will when you pull the trigger! Please, Randall! Don't do it!"

"Sorry, little bro."

"If you shoot that, you'll kill me, too!"

"You said it would hurt a lot. Not kill."

"Randall—"

"I love you, Josh."

Josh was about to scream *NO!* but someone beat him to it.

It was Grandma! Fighting her way through the wall of zombies, reaching for the TCD9 and taking it from Randall's hands.

"How does this sucker work?"

"First trigger to fire, second to send the juice," Randall said. "But you can't..."

"Hogwash," Grandma said. "Every single day I went to work, there was a chance I wouldn't make it home. I was willing to give my life, to save strangers. But you boys... you're not strangers. You're my family. And it isn't every day, a woman has the honor of saving her family. Tell my daughter that the three of you are the best things that ever happened to me."

She pulled the first trigger, and the spike springs fired and stuck into the wet ground at the barn doorway.

"I love you, very much," she said.

Grandma smiled.

She winked.

And then she pulled the trigger, and the whole world exploded with light.

Outside Einstein's Barn…

Oh, yeah. The safety catch on the roof.

Clevis picked up a decent rock, took aim, and threw it—

—the rock sailed through the air, hitting its target with a *CLANG!*

Then there was a blinding light, followed by darkness.

Inside The Barn

Once the hatch opened—good old Clevis!—Einstein squirted flame at the chute and the flying chair took off like a rocket—

—and immediately burst into flames. Just like it had done when Clevis tried it.

The giant, burning fireball of death that was comprised of Einstein and his wife shot right through the roof.

Clevis was right. Burning to death was a turble way to go.

Happily, the pain wouldn't last much longer, because Einstein's parachute had instantly combusted and they hurtled toward the ground at about a hundred miles an hour.

In Mr. Einstein's Cabin…

Josh had been correct.

It hurt. A lot.

He'd also been correct about it working. The geriatric zombies had all been thrown to the floor by the TCD9's shockwave, but they were getting back up, and none of them made any attempt at trying to eat us.

"Start the bucket brigade," I yelled at them. Then I went to Josh. He was kneeling next to our grandmother. She'd saved us, and the town, and possibly the whole world.

But it had come at a terrible cost.

"Is Grandma gonna be okay, Randall?"

My brother's brown eyes were wide with worry.

Grandma's brown eyes were fixed on…

Nothing. They stared into space. Blank.

Dead.

"I don't know, Josh."

I checked to see if her chest was moving.

It wasn't.

I knelt next to Grandma, feeling for a pulse I knew wasn't there. Then I interlaced my fingers and placed my palm on her sternum to begin CPR chest compressions.

"She can't die," Josh said, the tears streaming down his face. "Don't let her die, Randall."

One and two and three and four and—

Josh grabbed her hand. "Wake up, Grandma! You have to wake up!"

—five and six and seven and eight and—

I felt a hand on my shoulder. Mildred Kanipple, looking so, so sad.

"It's done," she said. "Let her go."

I felt my whole body sag. Like a balloon that had been deflated.

This wasn't how it was supposed to end. There was supposed to be a happy ending.

Where was the happy ending?

I stood up, unable to stop the tears. Miss Kanipple gave me a kind pat on the shoulder.

"She was a decent woman, your grandmother. And I never said it to her face, but she made me a better person. She forced me to try harder. And I'm going to miss her."

Josh was crying so hard he was about to fall over. I put my arm around him.

"I'll make you boys a promise," Miss Kanipple said. "Though I can never replace your grandma, whenever you come to Lake Niboowin, I'll bake you cookies."

"Like hell you will."

We turned. Grandma was sitting up.

Josh and I ran to her.

Then there was a whole bunch of laughing and hugging.

And a minute later, Mom and Dad ran in, and there was even more laughing and hugging.

It turned out to be a pretty happy ending after all.

With Debs, Floating in His Above Ground Pool…

Ha ha!" Einstein hooted, slapping the water. "And you said this pool was stupid, because we lived on a lake! This stupid stagnant pit of mosquito larvae just saved our lives! What do you think of that, Debs?"

"Shut up, Rupert."

Grandma's Cabin
Two Days Later...

As Mr. Einstein supervised, Deonte, Bob, Gustav, and Clevis installed Grandma's new garage door. Like the rest of us, they were wrapped in an assortment of bandages. But it didn't hinder their garage-door-installing abilities.

"Not bad for a group of retirees," I said as I watched.

Grandma tussled my hair. "Not bad for any age," she said. "Just because a person is retired, or elderly, or even in a nursing home, it doesn't mean they've worn out their usefulness."

"Do you feel the same way about Mildred Kanipple?" I asked.

"Funny thing. I couldn't stand that woman. But I think this whole experience might have finally ended our long-standing rivalry."

"Really?"

Grandma snorted. "Of course not. I'm wiping the floor with that old bat, next Bake-Off."

We went back into Grandma's cabin. Mom and Dad were in the hallway, getting all kissy face.

"Easy, you two," I said as I passed. "I don't need another little brother."

"How about a little sister?" Mom asked, grinning.

Dad raised an eyebrow. "Are you serious?" he asked her.

"Hell, no," Mom said. "Two is enough."

They laughed, then went back to smooching.

"Cookies are almost ready," Grandma said. The smell in her kitchen was nothing short of magical. "Go tell your brother."

I walked out onto the porch. The day was gorgeous. Blue skies, not too hot, the lake a giant mirror. It was the last day of vacation, and I felt conflicted. Sad, because I didn't want to leave here. And happy, because we'd avoided a geriatric zombie apocalypse with not even one single death.

Josh was on the pier, casting Dad's Musky Prowler into the lake. He was determined to catch the elusive fish of 10,000 casts before we went home.

By my count, he still had about 9500 to go.

"Cookies are ready," I said, standing next to him.

"You know nobody is going to believe us when we go to school," he said. "There's no proof any of it ever happened."

"I know."

Yesterday, the police and Homeland Security (apparently Mom had said something about terrorists) swept the area and didn't find any other zombies. The TCD9, thanks to Josh's calculations, had cured them all. The media blamed the whole incident on mass hysteria. The hundred-plus people who'd been bitten were given rabies shots to be on the safe side. None of the infected elderly protested. Apparently there was a bit of guilt related to them trying to eat two children, and they all preferred to keep that to themselves.

"So what do we tell our friends?"

I clapped him on the shoulder. "Tell them you finally learned how to swim."

"I could do that. But what I'd really like to tell them is that I caught a—"

Josh yelped, and pulled hard on his fishing pole. I thought he was faking it. But when I saw the rod bend nearly in half, I knew it was the real deal.

Only one fish could pull that hard. My younger brother had hooked a musky.

"Keep your tip up," I told him. "Adjust the drag. Let him some line."

I turned to head for the boat, docked next to us.

"Where are you going?" Josh said, panicked.

"To get the net."

"Don't leave me! I can't do this alone!"

"You can do this, Josh."

"What if I lose it?"

"Then you lose it. And catch another one, some other day. And when you do, I'll be there. I'll always be there for you. Okay?"

He nodded.

"Let the fish come to you," I told him. "Take it slow and easy. You got this."

Then I went to grab the net.

THE END

Joe and Talon Konrath Discuss Writing GRANDMA?

Joe: A bit of background. I had a tough time launching a writing career, collecting more than five hundred rejections over a ten year period before earning a dime. So when my son, Talon, expressed an interest in writing, I didn't encourage it. I didn't want him to go through all the hardships I did.

But when he turned sixteen and was fiddling around with this zombie story idea, I read it and really liked the premise. And I loved the character of Einstein. So I offered to collaborate and publish it.

Talon: It was a dream come true… until the editing began.

Joe: Yeah, there was a lot of editing. And rewriting. Talon is a lot better than he was three years ago, but he still has a lot to learn. (If it matters, I wasn't any good until I was about twenty-five.) But we stuck with it, made it kind of a hobby project. We even self-pubbed the first fifty pages a while ago, though that's been extensively rewritten since then.

Talon: My apologies to anyone who bought the first two parts and have been left hanging for several years.

Joe: The writing took as long as it took. Talon had school, and various fast food jobs. I was working on my own stuff. He would write a section, I'd edit and give him tips, he'd revise.

Talon: That was the cycle. A very tough cycle. It went like this: I'd write a whole page, re-read dozens of times, tweak words, shorten sentences, add action, and then he'd read it and tell me a hundred things wrong with my first word.

This went on and off throughout high school, and I have improved a bit since. It's more hard work than talent.

Joe: At the end of 2016, three years from when we first started, we sat down together and finished the book.

So a lot of this writing is mine. But this has Talon all over it. The characters, basic plot, a lot of the jokes; they're his. How'd you think up this idea, making a zombie story with retirees?

Talon: I love anything related to zombies. Books, TV, movies, but have never seen one where zombies talk, or were exclusively elderly. When I began writing a horror story about two brothers, a question struck me. What if my grandmother became a zombie? And what if she tried to eat me? That became; what if a horde of people over sixty-five became zombies?

Joe: Without trying to beat the reader over the head with themes, part of what drew me to this story is how the elderly are treated by society, especially in the USA. There are a lot of negative stereotypes about older folks, and it was fun to bust some of those.

There are also a few classic zombie movie references in GRANDMA?, which were fun to slip in.

Talon: *Night of the Living Dead*, obviously. Our ending was an homage to that classic, being trapped in a building surrounded by zombies. And the line, "They're coming to get you, Barbara."

Joe: I snuck in a few others as well.

For my longtime readers, this story takes place on Lake Niboowin (which is the Chippewa word for *dead*) in the fictional town of Spoonward. My previous novels RUM RUNNER and WEBCAM are also set there. Spoonward is up in the Burnett/Wabash County area, where I've been vacationing every year since I was two, and where I've taken Talon every year since he was still in his mom's tummy. Is that why you set this in Wisconsin?

Talon: Of course, it's the setting I know best. Being in a boat on a lake. Fishing. Swimming. Walking in the woods.

Joe: I remember that some of your earlier drafts were pretty violent, and I talked you out of a lot of that because we were making this young adult. Not that YA can't get violent, but you wrote parts like they were from a Lucio Fulci film.

Talon: Yeah, I think I had Grandma rip out Josh's intestines and then cackle while Randall watches in horror. And I had Einstein use his collection of invented weapons to slaughter hordes of elderly undead. The TCD9 was supposed to zap zombie bones to mush.

Maybe not the best idea for the genre...

Joe: I've ripped out plenty of intestines in my novels. But I don't think that was needed in this story. We've got heroes who are still kids, and a lot of funny scenes with supporting characters. I didn't think the tone supported over-the-top gore.

Talon: Name a zombie movie without incredible amounts of blood and brains! C'mon!

Joe: I can name a few. *Night of the Comet*, *Children Shouldn't Play With Dead Things*, *Omega Man*, *Sugar Hill*. I remember a movie called *One Dark Night* which was only PG, but it probably shouldn't have been.

I'd rate GRANDMA? PG-13. We managed to slip some gross stuff in.

Talon: Speaking of movies, my father and I have created a blog about the worst movies of all time. If you have a taste for wasting time, torturing yourself, or laughing uncontrollably, give it try, here: http://bestworstmoviesever.blogspot.com

Joe: We're watching what are considered the worst movies ever. Box office bombs. IMDB Bottom 100. Zero percent on Rotten Tomatoes. And then explaining why others should watch them.

So, are you going to continue writing stories?

Talon: Yes, this was a lot of fun to do, and I get very excited whenever someone buys a copy. I'm honored and very lucky to have J.A. Konrath as my dad.

Even if he sometimes smells like cheese.

Joe: That's because I eat a lot of cheese. It isn't a hygiene issue.

Talon: Why is there a shampoo bottle labeled "Cheese" in the shower?

Joe: Don't touch it. That's mine.

Thanks everyone for reading! If you liked it, please leave a review. Maybe Talon and I will write something else together in the future. If we get started now, it'll be ready in 2021.

Talon: Hey! I'll be good by then, right?

Joe: Sure you will, son.

Talon: Hooray!

Joe: Eat your hearts out, Stephen King and Joe Hill…

JOE KONRATH'S COMPLETE BIBLIOGRAPHY

JACK DANIELS THRILLERS

WHISKEY SOUR
BLOODY MARY
RUSTY NAIL
DIRTY MARTINI
FUZZY NAVEL
CHERRY BOMB
SHAKEN
STIRRED with Blake Crouch
RUM RUNNER
LAST CALL
SHOT OF TEQUILA
BANANA HAMMOCK
WHITE RUSSIAN
OLD FASHIONED
SERIAL KILLERS UNCUT with Blake Crouch
LADY 52 with Jude Hardin
65 PROOF short story collection
FLOATERS short with Henry Perez
BURNERS short with Henry Perez
SUCKERS short with Jeff Strand
JACKED UP! short with Tracy Sharp
STRAIGHT UP short with Iain Rob Wright
CHEESE WRESTLING short with Bernard Schaffer
ABDUCTIONS short with Garth Perry
BEAT DOWN short with Garth Perry
BABYSITTING MONEY short with Ken Lindsey
OCTOBER DARK short with Joshua Simcox
RACKED short with Jude Hardin
BABE ON BOARD short with Ann Voss Peterson
WATCHED TOO LONG short with Ann Voss Peterson

PHINEAS TROUTT THRILLERS

DEAD ON MY FEET
DYING BREATH
EVERYBODY DIES

STOP A MURDER PUZZLE BOOKS

STOP A MURDER – HOW: PUZZLES 1 – 12

STOP A MURDER – WHERE: PUZZLES 13 – 24

STOP A MURDER – WHY: PUZZLES 25 – 36

STOP A MURDER – WHO: PUZZLES 37 – 48

STOP A MURDER – WHEN: PUZZLES 49 – 60

CODENAME: CHANDLER SERIES

EXPOSED with Ann Voss Peterson

HIT with Ann Voss Peterson

NAUGHTY with Ann Voss Peterson

FLEE with Ann Voss Peterson

SPREE with Ann Voss Peterson

THREE with Ann Voss Peterson

FIX with F. Paul Wilson and Ann Voss Peterson

RESCUE

THE HORROR COLLECTIVE

ORIGIN

THE LIST

DISTURB

AFRAID

TRAPPED

ENDURANCE

HAUNTED HOUSE

WEBCAM

DRACULAS with Blake Crouch, Jeff Strand, and F. Paul Wilson

HOLES IN THE GROUND with Iain Rob Wright

THE GREYS

SECOND COMING

THE NINE

GRANDMA? with Talon Konrath

WILD NIGHT IS CALLING short with Ann Voss Peterson

CLOSE YOUR EYES

FOUND FOOTAGE

TIMECASTER SERIES

TIMECASTER

TIMECASTER SUPERSYMMETRY

TIMECASTER STEAMPUNK

BYTER

EROTICA
(WRITING AS MELINDA DUCHAMP)

FIFTY SHADES OF ALICE IN WONDERLAND
FIFTY SHADES OF ALICE THROUGH THE LOOKING GLASS
FIFTY SHADES OF ALICE AT THE HELLFIRE CLUB
WANT IT BAD
FIFTY SHADES OF JEZEBEL AND THE BEANSTALK
FIFTY SHADES OF PUSS IN BOOTS
FIFTY SHADES OF GOLDILOCKS
THE SEXPERTS – FIFTY GRADES OF SHAY
THE SEXPERTS – THE GIRL WITH THE PEARL NECKLACE
THE SEXPERTS – LOVING THE ALIEN
THE SEVEN YEAR WITCH

ORIGIN

Thriller writer J.A. Konrath, author of the Lt. Jack Daniels series, digs into the vaults and unearths a technohorror tale from the depths of hell…

1906–Something is discovered by workers digging the Panama Canal. Something dormant. Sinister. Very much alive.

2009–Project Samhain. A secret underground government installation begun 103 years ago
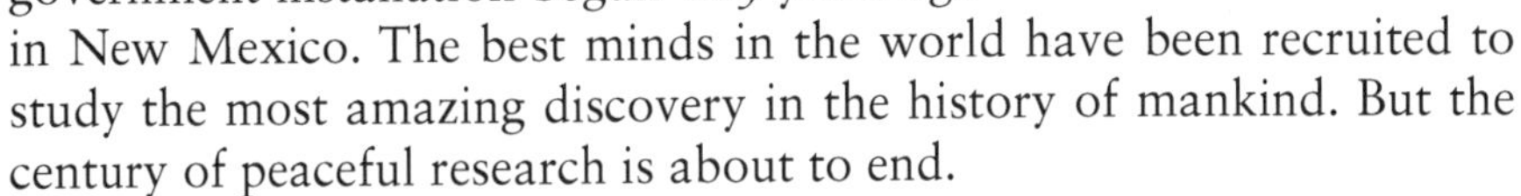
in New Mexico. The best minds in the world have been recruited to study the most amazing discovery in the history of mankind. But the century of peaceful research is about to end.

Because it just woke up.

When linguist Andrew Dennison is yanked from his bed by the Secret Service and taken to a top secret facility in the desert , he has no idea he's been brought there to translate the words of an ancient demon.

He joins pretty but cold veterinarian Sun Jones, eccentric molecular biologist Dr. Frank Belgium, and a hodge-podge of religious, military, and science personnel to try and figure out if the creature is, indeed, Satan.

But things quickly go bad, and very soon Andy isn't just fighting for his life, but the lives of everyone on earth…

ORIGIN by J.A. Konrath

All hell is about to break loose. For real.

THE LIST

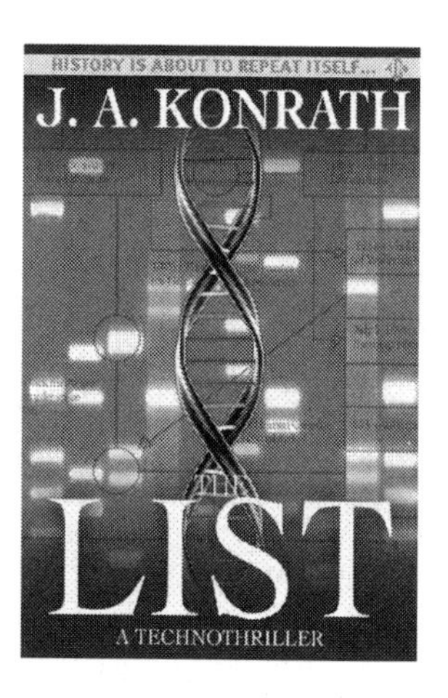

A billionaire Senator with money to burn…

A thirty year old science experiment, about to be revealed…

Seven people, marked for death, not for what they know, but for what they are…

THE LIST by J.A. Konrath

History is about to repeat itself.

WHISKEY SOUR

Lieutenant Jacqueline "Jack" Daniels is having a bad week. Her live-in boyfriend has left her for his personal trainer, chronic insomnia has caused her to max out her credit cards with late-night home shopping purchases, and a frightening killer who calls himself 'The Gingerbread Man' is dumping mutilated bodies in her district.

While avoiding the FBI and its moronic profiling computer, joining a dating service, mixing it up with street thugs, and parrying the advances of an uncouth PI, Jack and her binge-eating partner, Herb, must catch the maniac before he kills again...and Jack is next on his murder list.

WHISKEY SOUR is the first book in the bestselling Jack Daniels series, full of laugh-out-loud humor and edge-of-your-seat suspense.

Made in the USA
Columbia, SC
22 November 2017